I Love God But Church Stinks

AF808018

By
Phillip K Clark

Ebook ISBN: 978-1-964656-51-9
Paperback ISBN: 978-1-964656-52-6
Hardback ISBN: 978-1-964656-53-3

Contents

Introduction i

Growing up in the Church 1

Sin in the Church 10

Lack of Knowledge 22

Lack of Love 35

Lack of Holiness 43

Lack of Peace 48

Lack of Teaching 53

Lack of Wisdom 63

Lack of Faith 74

Lack of Understanding 80

The spirit of formality 89

Introduction

First, I would like to thank my Lord and Savior, Jesus Christ for giving me the courage to address the 21st century church. Does church stink? Of course, not. The church is the body of Christ. What stints is the 21st century church system, the false traditions, false doctrine, and false rituals that men have put into place. It is so unfortunate that evil men and imposters in the pulpits of the modern-day church are growing worse and worse, as they continue to deceive many while they themselves are being deceived. We seem to have churches on every corner of our cities and there is more chaos than ever. You don't have to drive far in the rural areas, and you will see church after church. It is so unfortunate that the church has allowed satan to infiltrate our buildings and introduce us to a god that does not line up with what is written in the Scriptures.

I'm saddened that I have witnessed pastors become CEOs and the church has become big business. It is more important to raise money than it is to save souls. I'm also saddened how the church proved to be under the sway of the wicked one (1 John 5:19) when it allowed the satanic government to shut its doors for months, and some are still shut down and will never reopen, during the COVID-19 pandemic (plandemic). After preaching faith for many years, and after telling members, "For God has not given us a spirit of fear, but of power and of love and of a sound mind." What an opportunity wasted to prove to the world our faith and trust in our great God and Savior, Jesus Christ. We must repent and ask God to have mercy on our churches and pray for men who are filled with His Holy Spirit will stand up and preach truth in these last days. Time is running out. We may be the generation to witness the return of Jesus the Lamb that was slain. I pray that as you read this book God will open your eyes and enlighten your mind to know that change is necessary. Holiness and righteous living are required before sanctification can truly come, and that sweet holy aroma will reach the nostrils of God and He will save the church and its members from the wrath to come.

Growing up in the Church

The time is 7:30 am Sunday, and the call comes up the stairs loud and clear. "Get Up, it's time to get ready to go to church," which meant Sunday school. My mother was very serious, and my three sisters and I knew it. She had two different tones when she spoke, and we as children knew the difference. My Uncle Felt would pick us up in front of the house at about 9:00 am and off we would go to Asbury Chapel A.M.E. Church in Waynesburg, Ohio. My uncle was a very good Sunday school teacher, but as a child, I never heard the good news of the gospel. We had a time which was allotted in the class where we had to quote a Bible verse. You may find this to be amazing, but several of us had the ability to memorize John 11:35 "Jesus wept."

It was a typical Sunday school class. The only reason most of us attended was because our parents made us attend. We heard that Jesus died on the cross and on the third day He rose, but the basic foundations of the Christian faith were kept from us. The part about receiving Jesus as your personal savior, Jesus dying for your sins, living holy, the Holy Spirit, living in darkness, and overcoming the flesh, were just a few of the subjects never mentioned. Therefore, the results of not hearing the truth of the gospel of Jesus Christ resulted in a lot of years that I would call wilderness living.

Wilderness living is a period in a person's life when they are on their own spiritually. When a person is on his or her own spiritually, they don't realize that they are separated from God, and they lack the ability to discern good from evil. Someone may have a knowledge of Jesus and associate Him with the church but don't know what it means to have a relationship with Him or know who He truly is, and lack knowledge of how much they truly need Him for directions in their life. Then most importantly, there is just a lack of knowledge that He came to die for our sins, and He wants to be our Lord and Savior.

Some consequences come with the decision to do life without Jesus. It really doesn't matter how much we attend church. If Jesus is not your Lord and Savior, you are on your own. I love the fact that the Bible says, "that while we were yet sinners Christ died for us." (Romans 5:8) But I appreciate and get satisfaction from Ephesians 2:4 "But God, who is rich in mercy, because of His great love with which He loved us, even when we were dead in trespasses, made us alive together with Christ. (By grace you have been saved)" That period of our lives when we are dead in our trespasses and sin is wilderness living. The sad part is that there are so many people who attend churches all over the world who are dead in their trespasses and sins and church members at the same time. I have just defined the life of most of you reading this book and probably most people you know who attend a church service weekly.

The problem is that holy and righteous living is not taught or put on display in most churches we choose to attend. The church has gotten away from the church in the book of Acts which details the church and its beginnings. People were saved by the thousands daily. The apostles boldly taught truth and were arrested for obeying God rather than man. The Apostle Paul was beaten, stoned, whipped, and thrown in prison on numerous occasions but refused to deviate from obeying God and preaching truth. He understood his purpose, and his calling when he wrote in Colossians 1:28, "Him we preach, warning every man in all wisdom, that we may present every man perfect in Christ Jesus."

The gospel of Jesus Christ is a mystery that was hidden for centuries but has been revealed to the saints. It has been revealed to true followers of Jesus Christ. Those who have been born-again. God wanted it that way. The mystery is Christ in you, His spirit living in you. He is the hope of glory. This hope of glory is a guarantee for every believer's future heavenly glory.

Paul writes in Colossians 1:26-28 The mystery which has been hidden from ages and generations but now has been revealed to His saints. To them, God willed to make known what are the riches of the glory of this mystery among the gentiles: which is Christ in you, the hope of glory. Him we preach, warning every man in all wisdom, that we may present every man perfect in Christ Jesus.

Now my uncle did teach us Old Testament stories. David and Goliath, Daniel and the lion's den, Adam and Eve in the garden, and many others. The question is, how was he to teach on spiritual issues when there was no one teaching holiness from the pulpit or no one in the pulpit living it out in front of him? Church service wasn't any more educating than Sunday school, just a formality. It was a rarity for us to start on time. What I most remember about church service is that husbands and wives who had been married for many years never sat together. Men on one side, and women on the other side, except my grandmother. She always sat three rows back behind my grandfather John, who sat up front with Mr. Cheeks. I believe they ran the church. Both seem to have been highly respected.

My father was probably one of the greatest gospel singers who never recorded an album. He along with Vera Kelly and Jeanette Stevens could bring most adults to tears on some songs they sang. But when Roy Williams and his wife Delouse would visit from Minnesota, the church would always call on him to play the piano and sing. I thought he was pretty good, but no one could sing better than my dad James Clark. He was the best. I can remember Daddy sitting in the choir stand looking over the congregation. It was like he could see everything at the same time. He was 6' 4" and weighed 250. My father could swing the meanest belt and I will never forget how it felt when he fulfilled his fatherly duties.

All the children sat together in the back of the church. We were for the most part pretty good kids. We weren't exposed to all that these children in the late 90s and early 21st century children are exposed to. Our parents put fear in us. I didn't understand why, but I appreciate it now more than ever, what they did and how they did it. My father would sit in the choir and look at us a certain way, and we knew we better get it together or else.

It seems every year or two we would be assigned another minister. Some could preach others couldn't. I didn't know the good from the bad, because I don't remember listening to any of the sermons. I only knew what little I heard adults speak about and it was very little. We weren't allowed in the same room that adults were conversing in. I assume the ones they liked could preach and the ones they didn't like couldn't. I do know that those who were assigned didn't teach much New Testament doctrine or biblical truth, if any because no spiritual transformation took place in the lives of my parents or other adults or any of the other children's parents who attended Asbury. None kept my attention or any of the children's attention who sat in the back. But what is apparent to me as I look back at my old church is an invitation to receive Jesus Christ as my personal Savior was never given. At the end of the preacher's sermons, we would always hear "The doors of the church are open." And if or when someone came forward it was an exciting time for the congregation. Another person they could hopefully count on to pay money to meet the demands of the district.

When people don't hear New Testament doctrine, or they consistently hear false doctrine, they celebrate something that is not worth celebrating. Let me explain. There is nothing wrong with a person deciding to join a church. The only reason why anyone should want to join a church is because divine doctrine is being taught, and the word is being rightly divided. The question is, are you joining the right church and are you joining for the right reason? The most important decision in life any of us can make is to repent and turn from our wicked ways and desire a new way of living by accepting Jesus

Christ as your Lord and Savior. This is more important than joining a church. As I look back at my church experience as a child, I don't remember ever being taught the importance of being saved. It was a non-issue then, and still is in most of our churches today. There is nothing more important to God than for all people to be saved. The Bible says that it is His desire for all men to be saved and come to the knowledge of the truth. (1 Timothy 2:4) Also angels rejoice in heaven when just one sinner comes to repentance. (Luke 15:10)

The families in town, of which there were two maybe three that I knew of who had the reputation of being saved, were looked upon as strange in the eyes of most of the people I knew. I assume it was just fear of the unknown. But as I think back and remember those families, they weren't like us. They led quiet and peaceable lives. The parents were nice people and the children kept to themselves and stayed away from us hoodlums. Most of the adults or children in the church I attended displayed very little to no knowledge of salvation or its importance. I know because it was never discussed at church or home. It's sad to say but, it just wasn't taught by the ministers of the church my family attended. Also, we weren't taught the importance of reading the Bible, the role of the Holy Spirit, or prayer. More important than that no one ever tried to live it out in front of us. We would attend church on Sunday morning and then go back to living a life that I know now, was not pleasing to God. Sunday school and church should be a time when people not only hear about our daily bread, but the bread we should be eating is the word of God. All our parents seemed to get along with one another and there never were any fights that I knew of between church members and their children. Disagreements I'm sure, but never anything physical. It was a typical neighborhood church that would meet on Sunday morning to have church service.

Now the pastors assigned to the church were not very spiritual either. Most of them smoked pipes, cigars, and cigarettes, and I even witnessed them indulging in alcoholic beverages after Sunday service. We had a preacher who would come to our home every Sunday after church. Before and after dinner he would sit down with my father and have a strong drink. Preachers then, like most preachers now, do what they do for the money. Drawing a check or making money must not be any man's purpose for pastoring a church. The number one priority of any pastor must be saving the souls of men. Preaching the truth in love. But that is a problem that most of these guys/gals have. They refuse to preach or teach the truth. You can't teach something that you do not know.

I believe a lot of that has to do with them not knowing the truth. Getting paid and how much is still on the minds of many preachers today, with no concern for the souls of men. That's why none of us thought of it as something wrong when we witnessed our parents and other adults unknowingly living destructive spiritual lives. It's a generational curse that can only be broken when a person hears the good news of the gospel of Jesus Christ and then comes to faith in Jesus Christ who leads you to the knowledge of the truth. That is why I understand why my church was uneducated when it came to spiritual matters. How could they teach their children, and we teach our children, and our children teach their children or how can any of them or any of us live a godly life if they or we weren't taught the truth, and no one lived it out in front of them or front of us? What's so bad about that is after all these years there are still so many people who attend Sunday school and church just for the sake of attending. Some are attending churches that their great-grandparents attended not realizing that they are on their way to hell with heaven on their mind. The importance of learning Scripture, having a consistent prayer life, and the importance of living a holy life is never discussed. In the church I grew up in, it was and probably still is more important to collect a claim, which is a dollar amount given to each church. Each church belongs to a district, that must raise a dollar amount and present it to a representative from the district or a presiding elder who may visit only to collect the money. The church is big business. That was and still is more important than the souls of the members. Talk about priorities, this system is from the pits of hell. That is another reason why people's lives aren't changed for the better. They keep sinning and falling into the snares of the devil, not learning anything about salvation or what God wants for their lives. "Ever learning, but never coming to the knowledge of the truth." 2 Timothy 3:7

When I think about that it saddens me, because people don't even realize that they are missing out on a relationship that raises above all relationships, and that is a relationship with the God of heaven through His Son Jesus Christ.

The church as we know it today stints. God is not pleased with how we conduct ourselves not only in church, but also outside the walls of the church. Men are not able to rightly divide the word. Neither do they have a desire to rightly divide the word. Ungodly men and women have crafted the use of false doctrine and a false Jesus to seduce the minds of people who have no knowledge of the true God or what scripture says.

An astonishing and horrible thing has been committed in the land: The prophets prophesy falsely, and the Priests rule by their own power and; my people love to have it so. But what will you do in the end? Jeremiah 5:30-31

The Bible was written to help believers overcome, any problem or difficult situation they are facing and will continue to face in life. More importantly, the Bible was written to save the souls of nonbelievers and to help believers grow spiritually in the faith.

"You, therefore, beloved, since you know this beforehand, beware lest you also fall from you own steadfastness, being led away with the error of the wicked; but grow in the grace and knowledge of our Lord and Savior Jesus Christ. To Him be the glory both now and forever. Amen." 2 Peter 3:17-18

People who attend church are so easily led away from the truth. We should know these things, but we spend very little time on our own learning who the true and living God truly is. Faith comes by hearing. It does not come from what you hear from a preacher who does not have your best interest at heart. We build our faith in God by hearing the word of God which is written on the pages of the holy scriptures, the Bible. These men and women standing in these pulpits are displaying the error of wickedness, leading people away from truth which Peter writes about in 2 Peter 2:17-19.

These are wells without water, clouds carried by a tempest, for whom is reserved the blackness of darkness forever. For when they speak great swelling words of emptiness, they allure through the lust of the flesh, through lewdness, the ones who have actually escaped from those who live in error. While they promise them liberty, they themselves are slaves of corruption; for by whom a person is overcome, by him also is brought into bondage.

This book is written to help all people see the church for what it has become. To show the members of the body of Christ the importance of spreading the love of Christ. Love is telling people the truth. The truth that is written in the scriptures. It is so unfortunate that the church has fallen for the lies of satan. He is the one speaking, the one performing through these weak unsaved church leaders. The so-called educated and the uneducated church leaders.

I am by no means stating that all churches operate or function like all the ones I've attended or grown up in.

The purpose of this book is to bring awareness to the misuse of people's time and money that has been going on in churches for centuries. The church was not created for people to be on display to receive glory and honor. It was set up to assemble people to worship God and give Him and our Lord and Savior Jesus Christ Praise and adoration for all the great things He and His Son have done and are doing.

Sin in the Church

Sin has been with us since the fall of man in Genesis chapter 3 when the devil deceived Eve. It was Adam's responsibility to protect her, but on this occasion, their roles were reversed, and Eve took the lead and was deceived by the devil. In the same way, the church has been deceived by the devil. We have allowed the devil and sin to take the lead in church service and we use and misuse the name of Jesus in order to feel legitimate about our church service.

The 21st-century church has become more and more like the world. Church used to be a light for the world. Now the world is a light for the church. There has never been a time more than now when the spirit of compromise has infiltrated the church like it has today. There is a spirit of seduction in the pulpits and congregations in most churches, denominational and non-denominational churches, and it is not addressed by most pastors. You cannot attend most churches without seeing breasts, booty, thighs, or the toolbox of men in tight pants and shirts. Pastors don't touch the subject of sin because they need to keep their business operating. Most would not dare to offend a paying church member. In the mega-church, it is all in your face. The pastor, pastor's wife, praise team leader, and most of the entire praise team, the choir, ushers, and it is not uncommon to be met at the door by a greeter cleaving.

There is a lot of unholy living in and out of the church by its members. It all starts with the pastor/preacher who in most cases refuses to touch the subject of sin. You can't have a righteous life or even attempt to live a righteous lifestyle until you deal with the subject of sin. The church has a responsibility to tell people that all have sin, and all have fallen short of the glory of God. (Romans 3:23) It is the reason why Jesus came to the earth.

Matthew 1:21 says, "And she will bring forth a Son, and you shall call His name Jesus, for He will save His people from their sins." The name Jesus means Savior. "The next day John saw Jesus coming toward him, and said, "Behold the Lamb of God who takes away the sin of the world." We need to be saved from our sins. That's our problem, and the church does not want to deal with it. 1 John 1:9 tells us, "If we confess our sins, He is faithful and just to forgive us our sins and cleanse us from all unrighteousness." Verse 8 says, "If we say we have no sin, we deceive ourselves, and the truth is not in us." If we never admit to being a sinner then salvation cannot take place in our lives. When preachers never discuss the subject of sin, they deny the existence of sin in their lives and the lives of people who attend the church service.

Sin destroys lives and leads people down a path of destruction. It is impossible to have a relationship with the God of heaven when you have sin in your life. Sin makes you unrighteous in the eyes of God, and the Bible says, "The wages of sin is death, but the gift of God is eternal life in Christ Jesus our Lord." (Romans 6:23) Jesus is God's gift to the world and is available to everyone who believes. It is so unfortunate that there are many who choose not to open the gift God is offering. Those who repent, believe the gospel, and obey Scripture are the ones who decided to open the gift.

It is so unfortunate that people attend church every Sunday and get so emotionalized and receive no direction on how to deal with the everyday issues of life. Scripture being taken out of context to grow membership and build legacies and earthly kingdoms which point people to the worship of idols. The worship of the pastor and so-called 1st lady, the worship of praise leaders and the praise team, and celebrity guests who have shown up in some churches I've been a member of. It is always what the pastor says and his interpretation of Scripture, as though a man has the last word and not the Bible. You hear Scripture in these churches, but the importance of the practice of Scripture is never reinforced. Church members are unable to lay aside the practice of sin. They are hearers of the word and not doers of the word.

"Therefore, lay aside all filthiness and overflow of wickedness, and receive with meekness the implanted word, which is able to save your souls. But be doers of the word, and not hearers only, deceiving yourselves." James 1:21-22

Notice that verse 21 does not say to lay aside some filthiness. It says to lay aside all filthiness and overflow of wickedness. This verse points to the evidence that most people in the church are not saved. James is writing to the church, not unbelievers. Most people find it difficult to do what the word of God tells them to do. People are deceived thinking that they can be saved without being a doer of the word. Obedience is the key to a successful spiritual life and lifestyle.

In Deuteronomy 30:15-19 the Bible says, "See, I have set before you today life and good, death and evil, in that I command you today to love the Lord your God, to walk in His ways, and to keep His commandments, His statutes, and His judgments, that you may live and multiply; and the Lord your God will bless you in the land which you go to possess. But if your heart turns away so that you do not hear, and are drawn away, and worship other gods and serve them, I announce to you today that you shall surely perish; you shall not prolong your days in the land which you cross over the Jordan to go in and possess. I call heaven and earth as witnesses today against you, that I have set before you, life and death, blessings and cursing; therefore, choose life, that both you and your descendants may live." God loves us so much that He not only gives us a choice, but He tells us what to choose. The problem is that people choose to be people pleasers instead of God pleasers. Caught up in the world and the things of the world. Refusing to let go of the pleasures of this life. "Do not love the world or the things of the world. If anyone loves the world the love of the Father is not in him." 1

John 2:15 Christians, churchgoers, and church members still drinking, smoking, cussing, using drugs, watching pornography, listening to music that does not edify God, people still on the milk of the Word unable to digest the solid food of the Word which makes it impossible to decern good from evil.

God tells us in verse 19 to choose life. Even though God is speaking to the children of Israel, these passages apply to us today. The life we must choose is a life with Jesus Christ. A life that must include obedience to God's word. There should be evidence of that obedience in your lifestyle. Most church members don't even know what God is offering because they don't spend any quiet time reading the Bible and praying. They only know what they are told in the Sunday morning church service.

The children of Israel refuse to keep God's commandments and spend most, if not all, of their lives in the wilderness or captivity, separated from God. Being involved in idol worship and practicing disobedience results in passive to severe wrath from the hands of God. The wages of sin separate us from God spiritually, and if you are separated from God, it means that you are spiritually dead while you live here on earth. For the wages of sin is death, but the gift of God is eternal life. (Romans 6:23) So, it shall be when you die, you shall be separated from Him for all of eternity. There is only one way to heaven and that is a life that is committed to Jesus Christ. Church membership, being a nice person, giving money to the poor, or even holding the highest office in the land will not get you into heaven if you don't believe what the Bible says about Jesus Christ and obey the word of God.

The Bible which is the Word of God, and the God of heaven has not only been taken out of the school but also the church. The problem is when it is used, it is misused or not used at all. The church should be a carry-over from Sunday school, which should be the basis fundamental teaching of the

Bible. The church should be a true worshipping experience of God's presence, which should include the admiration of His Son Jesus Christ with much thanksgiving and praise for all the great things He has done, and gratitude for the working of the Holy Spirit in your life. The teaching of God's holy word must be the most important part of the service. Done by a humble man filled with the Holy Spirit, who understands that he is only a tool or instrument God is using. He must realize that it is an honor and a privilege to stand before people that God loves, and he or she must teach the truth from the Bible. Sin and sinful thoughts get a church away from the true meaning of worship. There are in most services more emphasis on social and worldly events than spiritual issues.

Sin runs rampant throughout our society and has infiltrated the church in a way that has become the norm. You have so-called and self-proclaimed bishops and presiding elders who won't invite you to speak at their church because they don't want you telling their congregation about sin. A lot of that has to do with the sin in their lives and the money. Church is a multibillion-dollar business, and these pastors are dependent on the offerings that are taken up each time they meet: hustling, most times, poor people out of their hard-earned money. Preachers, who are in positions of authority, stand in approval of the sins of other preacher who have the responsibility of telling members about sin, and the tragedy of it. Preachers drink, smoke, cuss, use drugs, and abuse their position to make advances on women and men, and there are so many female preachers in churches today, which is unfortunate that men allow women to be out of order. The Bible is clear about the role of the woman in the church. "Let the woman learn in silence with all submission. And do not permit the woman to teach or to have authority over a man, but to be silence." 1 Timothy 2:11-12. "The older women, likewise, that they be reverent in behavior, not slanderers, not given to much wine, teachers of good things- that they admonish the young women to love their husbands, to love their children, to be discreet, chaste, homemakers, good, obedient to their own husbands, that the word of God may not be blasphemed." Titus 2:3-5

In some churches, there are an overwhelming number of females rather than males because of this spirit of role reversal. "But I fear, lest somehow, as the serpent deceived Eve by his craftiness, so your minds may be corrupted from the simplicity that is in Christ." 2 Corinthians 11:3 God's word is easy to understand. We have a problem in most churches today. The problem is this spirit of role reversal, which puts women over men. "But I want you to know that the head of every man is Christ, the head woman is man, and the head of Christ is God." (1 Corinthians 11:3) God is interested in His order, His way of doing things, not man's orders or traditions. It allows sin to flow from the pulpit to and through the congregation. In the pulpits, you have men who have lost the desire for their wives and take advantage of other females in and out of the church, and you have women who have lost the desire for their husbands and seek comfort from males in and outside of the church. Also, there is the problem of male and female preachers who lose the desire for the opposite sex and seek the same sex. You have single preachers who can't control their desires for sex and, if allowed, will take total advantage of men, women, singles, and married couples. You have men and women whose minds are perverted and desire to have sex with children in the church. When you have people in authoritative positions who lead a sinful life, that sinful spirit flows down through the congregation. The congregation has no one who sets a standard of righteous living. Everybody does what is right in their own eyes when you don't have a leader who lives a holy life. 1 John 3:4 states, "Whoever commits sin also commits lawlessness, and sin is lawlessness." Lawlessness is not keeping God's law. Most people who attend church ignore the laws of God.

Sin is simply bad behavior that is contagious, and if not quarantined, it spreads like wildfire, not only in church but in society. We don't have to look far to see how sin spreads. Look at our society. If you read Romans 1:18-32 it describes the America we live in today. Verse 18 says, "The wrath of God is revealed from heaven against all ungodliness and unrighteousness of men who suppress the truth in unrighteousness." We have a truth that is suppressed in the home, school, government, media, and, more tragically, in church. The church covers up or suppresses the wonderful attributes of God's love. Some churches don't teach that you must be born again so you can start a life without sin dominating it. The receiving of the Holy Spirit is suppressed. After you are born again, you need the Holy Spirit to help you with this new life in Jesus. It is a hold new way of living, a hold new way of life. You walk in the Spirit; you walk in the light of God's holy word.

God has programmed something inside of all humans that lets us know there is a God. That is why it says in verses 19-20, "because what may be known of God is manifest in them, for God has shown it to them. For since the creation of the world His invisible attributes are seen clearly by the things which are made, even His eternal power and Godhead so that they are without excuse." So even though they try to explain the existence of God away, it is a waste of time because deep down inside, we know, and they know it is a God. The problem is the unbelievers and church members refuse to give God the glory that only He deserves. Verse 22-23 says that "their foolish hearts were darkened (and still are darkened.) Professing to be wise they are fools." Which leads to idol worship.

Once truth is suppressed, men don't recognize God for who He is and create their own gods. They become unthankful and refuse to glorify God for who He is. It leads to unimaginable sins like homosexuality. Romans chapter 1 tells how women lose their desires for men, which leads to men losing their desires for women. "God gives them up to uncleanness, in the lust of their hearts, to dishonor their own bodies among themselves." (Roman 1:24) Verse 25 states, "They exchange the truth of God for a lie." I was born that way." "Not attracted to the opposite sex." "Always knew there was something different about me." The only difference is that there are a few people who desire to do all they can to obey God's word, and there are many people who desire not to obey. Is it really not that hard to figure out?

Both men and women are born with different equipment. Homosexuals and lesbians choose to misuse the equipment. There is no such thing as a homosexual. There is no such thing as a transgender. What you have is people who have lost their minds. They are under the influence of the spirit of darkness. They need to be delivered from a life that leads to destruction.

Once a society refuses to retain God in their knowledge (v.28), "God gives them over to a debase mind, to do those things which are not fitting." John Macarthur writes, "God has tested man's mind and has found them worthless and useless." When a society reaches this point, the Bible says it is "filled with all unrighteousness, sexual immorality, wickedness, covetousness, maliciousness; full of envy, murder, strife, deceit, evil-mindedness, they are whisperers, backbiters, haters of God, violent, proud, boasters, inventors of evil things, disobedient to parents, undiscerning, untrustworthy, unloving, unforgiving, unmerciful." But what is so sad about a society that chooses to practice sin is explained in verse 32. Who, knowing the righteous judgment of God, that those who practice such things are deserving of death not only do the same but also approve of those who practice them. The Bible explains that the people in charge of giving out the correct punishment don't. The question is, why? Well, it answers the question. Because they not only practice these same sins but also find it easy to approve of them. It is not only sad but sick. To think that we have people with debased minds writing laws and making important decisions for this country shows us the importance of prayer and praying for these men and women.

We cannot afford to give up on their salvation or the salvation of all people around the world. God is a God of the impossible, so we must continue to believe that God's word is able to change the hearts of men and women everywhere. He has set life and death before us, and we, as individuals, must make the right choice. So, where does an individual start? I am so excited you asked that question.

It all starts with repentance. It is the most important choice one can make when made aware of his or her sinful nature. What does it mean to repent? It starts with experiencing godly sorrow; it produces repentance that leads to salvation, not to be regretted, but sorrow of the world produces death. 2 Corinthians 7:10 There is a difference between godly sorrow and worldly sorrow. Godly sorrow produces a tremendous amount of sorrow over one's sin. Sorrow of the world is unrepentant sorrow that produces self-pity. It is the lifestyle of a person still involved in sin. You hate that you got caught sinning. I believe it could even lead to depression.

Repentance for me was coming to the realization that I was a rotten sinner, that God loved me so much that He gave all that He had to save me, His only precious Son, Jesus Christ. Realizing that it should have been me on that cross. But Jesus took my place. After staring godly sorrow in the face, it produced repentance. I looked back over my life and saw a rotten sinner. I was tired of living a life that was only going to take me to a place I feared most. That place was and is hell, and God offered me a way out. Godly sorrow produces repentance, which leads to salvation. At first, I thought all I had to do was confess that I was a sinner, believe in Jesus as my Lord and Savior, and believe God raised Jesus from the dead, and I would be saved. There is more to the story than just confessing and believing. The challenge was a decision to stop living in sin. When I made that decision to stop sinning, repentance took place in my life. I wanted to please the God of heaven. Matthew 4:17 states, "From that time Jesus began to preach and to say, repent for the kingdom of heaven is at hand." Mark 1:15 Jesus says, "The time is fulfilled, and the kingdom of God is at hand. Repent and believe the gospel." Repent therefore and be converted, that your sins may be blotted out, so that times of refreshing may come from the presence of the Lord. Acts 3:19

Repentance is when one decides to start on the road of recovery from a sinful life. It's when one makes up his or her mind that they are going to follow Jesus and not return to a life of sin. God spends time restoring you as you experience a period of recovery. It is like having surgery. The recovery is a spiritual experience unlike any other. The time you spend in recovery is refreshing because of the presence of the Lord. Some heal faster than others, but the healing period must take place so you can get out on the battlefield and fight the good fight of faith.

After that, you must choose to receive what has been made available for you, the Holy Spirit. He gives you the power to stop living a life of sin. The Holy Spirit is an enabler. If you smoke, He takes those desires away from you. If you use alcohol or drugs, He gives you the power to say no. If you cuss or use bad language, it is the Holy Spirit who moves in and changes you and puts a new language in your mouth. If your mind is perverted and you have a desire for the same sex, the Holy Spirit will take those desires away from you. Psalm 51 King David asked for God to have mercy on him because of the sin he had committed. Verse 10: "Create in me a clean heart, O God, and renew a steadfast spirit within me." The Holy Spirit gives a person the power they need to stop sinning. He gives him a fresh start in life by renewing a person's heart and thoughts.

The decision one makes to follow the Lord Jesus Christ is the best decision one will ever make, and part of the good news of the gospel is that one does not have to do it alone. We have a helper who is the Holy Spirit, who will comfort us on our journey as we grow in the knowledge of the truth. He also shows you the importance of praying and spending time alone with God through reading His Word. People lie and say that God speaks to them in an audible voice. God speaks to us through the Scriptures. I had to intentionally set some time aside to pray and read the Word. God opened a new world to me through His Word. I asked for wisdom, knowledge, and understanding of what I was reading. The Lord blessed me with discernment.

We all have heard this: You don't realize how important someone or something is until it is gone. Well, you won't realize how much you needed or need the Holy Spirit until you have Him. You have God living on the inside of you directing you in every area of your life. He is made available to us only if we choose to use Him. The problem is that we are not being taught such basic doctrine in most traditional churches. Most preachers can't get past the dramatics of Jesus dying on the cross, but early Sunday morning, He got up! Sweat was flying, spit was erupting, and handkerchiefs were waving, always sounding like something was stuck in their throat. And you always have someone saying "preach…" Just flesh on display with no desire to help the people, who are listening.

That is why it is so important for us to repent and ask God to forgive us of our sins and decide to follow the Lord Jesus Christ. So, we can be delivered from the power of sin and the consequences it brings. Sin continues to destroy the lives of so many people because of the power it has over our flesh. It is so unfortunate that our society promotes and values a sinful lifestyle. People get excited about sin because its mere existence excites the flesh. People enjoy sin and the practice of it. When we sin, we never take into consideration the consequences of it. The problem is the devil never shows us the downfalls or consequences of the decisions we make when we participate and continue to practice sin. It affects not only us but also the people around us who are impacted by these foolish decisions that we make when we willfully disobey Scripture. Our wives, children, parents, brothers and sisters, friends, and other family members are affected by our selfish decisions. Having sex outside of marriage is applauded and promoted in and outside the church. I don't remember any adult telling me when I was a kid to refrain from sexual activity. In school, we were taught sex education. You were made to feel like a failure if you didn't have a girlfriend that you could have sex with. During Sunday school and church, no one was teaching us kids the importance of remaining a virgin until you were married. I weep at the many times I tied myself sexually to a female other than my wife. Breaking the heart of God because of my desire to fulfill the lust of my flesh. But thank be to God, that while I was still a sinner, Christ died for an ungodly person like me. Delivering me and setting me free from a lifestyle of sin. And when I do sin, I have an advocate, a substitute that pleads my case to the Father, Jesus Christ. His blood cleanses me from all the sins in my life. I am only asked to repent and confess my sins. He is faithful and just to forgive me and clean me from all unrighteousness, not some unrighteousness. He cast our sins as far as the East is from the West. And never reminds us of them again. Now, that's a great, loving, and faithful God.

Lack of Knowledge

The church, as most of us know it today, stints, and God is not pleased with what is going on in most of the services that take place on Sunday morning, and it all starts with the lack of knowledge of God's word. Proverbs 1:7 says, "The fear of the Lord is the beginning of knowledge, but fools despise wisdom and instructions." The fear of the Lord means you have decided to take God seriously. There are many people who attend church but lack a reverential fear of God. God is not a God who wants you to come to Him shaking in your boots. He just wants what only He deserves. To be admired, esteemed, marveled, and obeyed. He is praiseworthy, and we should be in awe and in wonder of who He is. But fools despise godly wisdom and instructions not only from God but even from their parents or grandparents, who only want the best for them. What is the definition of a fool? A silly person, a person who lacks judgment or sense. A weak-minded or idiotic person. To act like a fool, joke, play.

Job 11:12 describes the fool and his desire to obtain wisdom and instructions. "For an empty-headed man will be wise when a wild donkey's colt is born a man." In most churches, when we do not receive godly instructions from the pulpit, we make foolish decisions and bad choices that lead to bad consequences. There are some people who have attended church all their lives and still are not saved. They are totally unaware of the importance of being saved. It's difficult to imagine the number of people who have died and gone to hell, even though they were church members all their lives and maybe even held important offices in the churches they attended because they never heard the gospel message. They, like I, never knew how much God loved me until I heard the message. Church members live miserable lives because they never experience the love of God. They're unable to love not only others but also themselves. They love the world and the things of the world but not God. The Bible says, "If you love Me, keep My commandments." (John 14:15). "If you keep My commandments you will abide in My love, just as I kept My Father's commandments and abide in His love. (John 15:10) (the Me, refers to Jesus Christ, the King of kings and the Lord of lords)

Jesus said to those Jews who believed in Him, "If you abide in My word, you are my disciples indeed. And you shall know the truth, and the truth shall make you free." (John 8:31-32) In order for any of us to learn about something or someone that draws our interest, we must invest time in that someone or something we are interested in. When we develop feelings for someone, we do not find it difficult to find time to spend with that person. The only reason why we do not spend time with God is because we don't develop feelings for Him. The important word in verse John 8:31 is "if". The word if is a conjunction. In verse 31, Jesus could be asking if that is the case or granted that if you make the effort to abide, or will you make the decision to abide.

We must understand the importance of abiding. The importance of knowing and understanding the truth is essential. We must get understanding to the point in our life that we realize because we have decided to abide, this truth is making us free. Then, there is so much to be discovered as you abide or hang out with Jesus. Churchgoers like to hang out around the church, just like some of the Jews hung out around Jesus, but there was always and still is an inability to develop a desire for the truth. Jesus not only taught the truth, but He lived the truth, and He explained to them that He hung out with His Father and His Father instructed Him on how to conduct Himself. He further explained their actions were self-explanatory to Him because they conducted themselves like their father, the devil. If we are not receiving instruction from God (the Holy Spirit), then we are receiving instructions from the devil, and that makes us children of the devil. A lack of spiritual knowledge in anyone's life brings about a lot of challenges that can be avoided if there is someone willing to not only teach but demonstrate a life that abides in Jesus Christ.

If you have a pastor or spiritual leader who lives a life that exemplifies a life that loves the Lord Jesus Christ, and if he realizes the importance of obedience, please don't take that for granted. Pray for that person and encourage them to continue the good fight of faith.

Another fact about knowledge is that it starts with belief. One must believe in the Lord Jesus Christ, who promises believers eternal life. The new birth takes place, which gives you the ability to love others, believers, and non-believers. Also, a desire to obey and keep His commandments laid out in the Bible. The results of this type of belief help believers deal with and learn how to obtain victory in the everyday issues of life. "Whoever believes that Jesus is the Christ is born of God, and everyone who loves Him who begot also loves him who is begotten of Him. By this, we know that we love the children of God, when we love God and keep His commandments. For this is the love of God, that we keep His commandments. And His commandments are not burdensome. For whatever is born of God overcomes the world. And this is the victory that has overcome the world-our faith. Who is he who overcomes the world, but he who believes that Jesus is the Son of God." (1 John 5:1-5)

Once we begin to believe what is written in the Bible, knowledge is established. Remember, Jesus said, "If you know the truth." Oh, how important it is to obtain knowledge of the new birth. Jesus tells Nicodemus in John chapter 3, "You must be born again." Once you believe and start to obey, faith kicks in. Faith is confidence or truth in a person or thing: faith in another's ability. Placing one's faith in the Lord Jesus Christ and the doctrines or teachings of the Bible, a believer starts to obtain knowledge of the promises of God. Also, you learn the importance of placing confidence in the God of the Bible and not oneself.

The apostle Paul writes in Titus 1:1-3, "Paul, a bondservant of God and a apostle of the Lord Jesus Christ, according to the faith of God's elect and the acknowledgment of the truth which accords with godliness, in hope of eternal life which God, who cannot lie, promised before time begin, but has in due time manifested His word through preaching, which was committed to me according to the commandment of God our Savior."

God makes these precious promises to those who make the decision to believe what is written in His word. Paul explains God cannot lie. In Numbers 23:19, the Bible says, "God is not a man, that He should lie; nor a son of man, that He should repent. Has He said, and will He not do? Or has He spoken, and will He not make it good?" Reading and believing these verses makes it easier for a person to place his or her faith in the God of the Bible. Acknowledgment of the truth will cause a person to line up one's life with the word of God, which all points to the life of God's Son, Jesus Christ. Knowing the importance of the death and resurrection and the saving truth puts a person on the path of righteous and godly living. Paul says truth agrees with godliness and eternal life. Also, it is important to notice how Paul humbled himself and allowed God to manifest His word through him by preaching truth and sound doctrine. Paul's assignment was to place beyond doubt any unbelief that one might be experiencing. He warned and taught against the false teaching that was taking place and ordered others to sharply rebuke those who brought that kind of teaching/preaching to the church.

Some churches never teach or preach on the importance of the new birth, receiving the Holy Spirit, loving Jesus Christ, loving others, living a godly life, keeping God's commandments, or the importance of living a victorious Christian life. After being saved and filled with the Holy Spirit, I've learned the importance of obedience to God's holy word. It has been a process, and it still is a process, but like anything else, the more I practice it, the better I get at it. I'm not perfect and never will be. Do I miss it sometimes? The answer is yes. But my desire is to live a life that will not cause others to stumble. Don't want anyone to continue struggling with the fundamentals of the Christian life. Also, to show all observing that the decision to make Jesus Christ my Lord and not just your Savior is the most rewarding decision I could ever make. Practicing righteousness is what I long for.

Great athletes in professional sports get better because they practice. Husbands and wives become better spouses when they practice biblical instructions on marriage. Trying to work hard at what the Bible says will make their marriage better. Teachers become better teachers if they put forth the effort it takes to make them better. As Christians, followers of Christ, and church members, we must put forth the effort to know the God of heaven and His holy word. Then, we can not only feel good about life but, more importantly, about eternity because life is all about eternity. Others want you to think it's something else, but that is not true. Going to heaven and missing hell throughout eternity is what everyone wants to do. Even the ones who say they don't believe in it. Going to church every Sunday, bringing a nice person, singing in the choir, being an usher, giving large amounts of money, sitting in a pulpit, or the fact that grandmamma prayed for you will not get you into heaven. Only knowing and trusting in what Jesus Christ did for you on the cross gets you in. That's why the theology of works or "work my way in" is a false belief system that has been put into the minds of so many people who attend church. There is nothing we can do while we are here on this earth to get us into heaven. Jesus is the only reason why anyone has entered or will enter heaven.

I know a few people who refuse to miss a church service or a church meeting, and there is nothing wrong with that if you feel you must. But the question is, has your life been transformed by the relationship you have developed with the Lord Jesus Christ? Or are you just going through the motions? We are not on a point system, and God is not keeping count. He just wants to know, while you were here and you had the chance, did you know My Son? Did you place your faith and trust in the works of Jesus Christ, My only begotten Son, who laid down His life so you could experience eternity? Were the things of this world more important to you than eternity? Did you spend any time allowing God to speak to you through His word? Did you seek answers to life's tough issues through prayer? Did your life or lifestyle help or hinder others who were watching? Did you put God first and love others? Did you say to yourself, what can I do to have an impact on the kingdom? We need to know the answers to these important questions while we are here on earth. In John 17:3, Jesus said, "And this is eternal life, that they may know You, the only true God, and Jesus Christ whom You have sent."

The Bible is clear in 1 Timothy 2:3-4 "For this is good and acceptable in the sight of God our Savior, who desires all men to be saved and to come to the knowledge of the truth." The problem we as church members have is written in 2 Timothy 3:7, "Always learning and never able to come to the knowledge of the truth." There is too much "taking church for granted." It's a ritual or tradition we go through on Sunday morning. Too much false doctrine, bad preaching and teaching, lack of knowledge, faith, hope, or trust in God's word. We listen to what Rev. Jones, Bishop Leroy, or Presiding Elder Smith has to say, and that's all we know. Ever learning from a man's point of view and never searching the Scriptures for yourself to see what God's word has to say. If we would just spend a little time and read the Bible, and if we just ask God to help us understand what we are reading, we will discover that we need to pray for Rev. Jones and all the others and get as far away from them as we possibly can and ask God to lead us not only to a Bible believing church but a pastor and a congregation who lives it out in front of you. It's called integrity. Integrity simply means an adherence to moral and ethical principles, soundness of moral character, and honesty. There is truly a lack of integrity in our world today.

At the same time, you must be careful. Just because a church uses the phrase "Bible believing church," it doesn't mean it is one. Some of these pastors/CEOs can and will twist Scripture that can fool the very elect. It sounds good and gets people excited but most of it doesn't line up with the Bible. They prey on the fact that there is a segment of people who feel the need to be involved in church and their lack of a desire to know and learn Scripture.

Scripture twisting is a tool of the devil, and some of these men are being used by the devil and fail to realize it because they are not saved and filled with the Holy Spirit. Just being religious or belonging to a religious organization is not appealing to God. Jesus was constantly confronted by the religious leaders of His day. They hated Him so much that they wanted to kill Him, and they did. People don't like hearing the truth. They will argue with you, debate you, and hate you because you don't agree with their way of thinking, which, in most cases, they are misinformed, or they are living a lie because they have not heard or experienced the truth.

God wants a relationship with every individual who desires to have one with Him. Remember, Jesus stands at the door and knocks. He is not serving a warrant for your arrest. He is not going to kick the door in. He is seeking a relationship. He wants you to realize the importance of being reconciled to God. "He made Him who knew no sin to be sin for us, that we might become the righteousness of God in Him." (2 Corinthians 5:21). You don't become the righteousness of God through a pastor, a bishop, a presiding elder or some so-called evangelist/prophet, that the church- going community has made a celebrity.

I was caught up in a church like that for eight years until God took those blinders off my eyes and helped me realize that I needed to get my family out of that church. Just because something sounds good or kind of makes sense to you, it doesn't make it right, or it doesn't mean it lines up with

Scripture. Just because a church is growing, that is not evidence that God is involved in the growth. People, especially the lost, will flock to a church where they are not challenged spiritually. If a pastor never deals with the sin issue, then people will revisit that church and eventually join. Sinners and some Churchgoers who have not made Jesus the Lord of their lives don't like to feel convicted for their lifestyle. They want to feel comfortable about their everyday way of life without hearing what the Lord God is saying when it comes to living the life of a true believer. They want Jesus to be their Savior, but not their Lord.

You live this Christian life and discover that obedience brings spiritual success. The more you obey God, the more He leads and guides you through this life. People listen and follow these ministers who can twist the Scriptures just enough to make you believe it because it sounds good. When Scripture is taught correctly, it should challenge and convict not only sinners but also saints.

Paul prayed for the saint in Ephesians 1:16, stating, "I do not cease to give thanks for you, making mention of you in my prayers." He continued in verses 17&18. "That the God of our Lord Jesus Christ, the Father of glory, may give you the spirit of wisdom and revelation in the knowledge of Him, the eyes of your understanding being enlighten, that you may know what is the hope of His calling, what are the riches of the glory of His inheritance in the saint." And he doesn't stop there. In verses 19&20 Paul continues, "and the exceeding greatness of His power toward us who believe, according to the working of His mighty power which He worked in Christ when He raised Him from the dead and seated Him at His right hand in heavenly places." Wow, that was a mouthful. A powerful prayer that we all can pray.

To come into the knowledge of Jesus Christ and receive this power that is made available, a person must first believe. Paul stated that it's toward those of us who believe. We must believe that God makes the power to live this Christian life available to those who are His. Once a believer understands this inheritance and the fact that we are inheriting resurrection power, then we're able to have spiritual success. It's not just a little power that God is making available for us, but it's the exceeding greatness of His power toward us. That's why the eyes of our understanding must be enlightened because there is a hope out there that we can hold on to.

The Bible is clear in John 4:23-24 "But the hour is coming, and now is, when the true worshippers will worship the Father in spirit and in truth; for the Father is seeking such to worship Him. God is Spirit, and those who worship Him must worship Him in spirit and in truth." Now, let us take a moment to understand the importance of what Jesus is saying here. It is one of the most important statements Jesus made when it comes to not only church service but also our lifestyle.

The worship of God for a true believer is 24/7 365. (24 hours a day, seven days a week, 365 days a year) People want God to meet them at the church on Sunday morning for one to two hours, help them feel a little better about themselves, and say, see you next week, God, and live like the world or worse. Jesus says, "But the hour is coming, and now is that "the true worshipper" (in verse 23.) The woman at the well, whom Jesus is speaking to in verses 7-26, can be compared to the average church member today. In verse 22, Jesus says, "You worship what you do not know." Most people who attend church attempt to worship a God that they do not know. Most people know that there is something important about attending church but don't realize the importance of true worship. True worship is a spiritual issue.

So, how does a person worship God in spirit and in truth? First, you must be saved. Then have knowledge of the role of the Holy Spirit. His job is to bring you to the knowledge of the truth, which points to the Lord Jesus

Christ, after you make the decision to receive Him as your personal Savior. Jesus says in verse 24, "God is Spirit, and those who worship Him must worship in spirit and in truth." If salvation and the receiving of the Holy Spirit have not taken place in your life, there is no true worship of God. No Holy Spirit, no true worship. Jesus says, "God is Spirit." Most people don't worship what they can't see. That is why Jesus spoke in parables. Most people who witnessed Jesus' miraculous sign and wonders still could not see that He was the Messiah whom the Jewish people had read and heard about was coming. He taught the truth, but they were unable to comprehend what He was saying. In Matthew 13:13, he said, "Seeing they do not see and hearing they do not hear." Most people just go through the motions when it comes to church service and worship. They're not interested in worshiping a God they cannot see. Churchgoers or non-believers' worship what they see. Even though some people claim to have seen spirits, the Bible says no one has seen God. People worship cars, houses, money, celebrities, professional athletes, children, parents, and all sorts of things they can see. And they don't even realize that idol worship is taking place when it comes to the time and effort put into getting to know these gods that they can see. That's why people have problems when someone close to them dies. They moan for days, months, or even years because the inevitable takes place. All of us are going to die. I'm not saying that people should not be sad when a loved one or friend dies. If your sadness tarries, it is possible that idol worship is taking place. There was a dependence there that was suddenly lost. A void that can only be filled by the Lord Jesus Christ Himself.

People just don't worship what they do not know. Jesus also says, "They must worship Him in spirit and in truth." The truth is something that most so-called Christians or churchgoers don't know. They've heard the story of how Jesus came to earth, died on the cross, and on the third day He rose. But what they failed to understand is how important the significance of the resurrection of Jesus Christ was.

If Jesus had not risen from the dead, it would take away the uniqueness of Christianity. Jesus being brought back to life makes Him and what true followers know and believe unique and different from all other religions. Jesus is alive, while all other gods and prophets are dead. The Bible says God raised Him from the dead and seated Him at His right hand in the heavenly places. (Eph. 1:20).

Also, that same power used to raise Jesus from the dead lives on the inside of us, giving us supernatural power to live out this Christian life. A lot of people who attend church lack knowledge of this power God has made available to us who believe in the death and resurrection of His Son. This lack of knowledge stems from years of not being taught the word of God by men and now men and women who lack this same knowledge needed for one to have spiritual success.

Your lifestyle should be a lifestyle of worship. Holiness and righteous living must be included in your everyday life. The reason why so many people don't attend church is because they are attracted by something or someone who is different. Most churchgoers can out smoke, out drink, out dance, and out curse them, and what that does is destroy your witness or make you unattractive spiritually. It's like a handsome man or an attractive woman with poor hygiene. They look great from a distance, but when you get close and see their smile, or they smell awful, you are immediately turned off. People who don't attend church need to see someone who is not like them. Someone they respect and admire because there is something different about them. Not someone who gives non-believers the impression that they are not approachable or unloving, and please don't give them the impression that you think highly of yourself. We must be believers who allow the Spirit of God to be on display actively.

The Bible says, "When you are in Christ, you are a new creation; old things pass away. Behold all things become new." (1 Cor. 5:17 NKJ) It does not say that some things become new, but all things. You can't pick and choose what you want to be new in your life. You must choose to leave that sinful life behind you and, with the help of the Holy Spirit, proceed to a lifestyle of godliness and live in obedience to God's word. Worshipping God in spirit and truth not only involves Sunday morning worship but also a lifestyle that attracts unbelievers to God. People must see that you are different. You can't return to that old way of doing things. For all of us, it's a process. The more you practice godliness and righteousness, the better you get at living that kind of lifestyle. You may stumble from time to time, but God is a forgiving God, and Jesus paid the price for your sins by dying on the cross. You just tell God what you did (repent), and you keep your focus on Jesus. 1 John 1:9 says, "If we confess our sins, He is faithful and just to forgive us of our sins and to cleanse us from all unrighteousness."

Philippians 1:6 says, "Being confident of this very thing, that He who has begun a good work in you will complete it until the day of Jesus Christ."

Once you have truly given your heart to the Lord Jesus Christ, He is the one responsible for the work of salvation, the cleansing of your past life, and the beginning of an extraordinary new life with the God of heaven.

Most churches don't teach all that this Christian life has to offer. It robs people of a life of peace and spiritual insight into the world. The church that doesn't teach basic Bible principles is lining itself up with the world and the god of this world, the devil, whose goal is to be your god while you think the God of heaven is. He has infiltrated the church and taken it to levels where his spirit holds most of the important positions in the church. Most people are following a system that was set up by him and continues to grow in ways that only the Bible could have predicted. It is so easy to get caught up in because people refuse to obtain the knowledge necessary for deliverance. Knowledge of God's word is the key to having a successful spiritual life. The great thing about the Bible is that you don't have to dig far before you discover God's love, grace, and mercy He provides through His Son Jesus Christ.

Proverbs 9:10 says, "The fear of the LORD is the beginning of wisdom, and knowledge of the Holy One is understanding."

The next time you pick up your Bible, you want to understand what you are reading. It starts with knowing who God is. He is the Father of our LORD and Savior Jesus Christ. He is the one that came to this earth to save us from our sins and to give us life and life more abundantly. Understanding will come if you obtain biblical knowledge in your heart and mind.

Lack of Love

Love is not only something we, as humans, want, but it is something that we, as humans, need and seek. So why is there a lack of love in the church? Because there is very little to no truth taught about love. People who love you, tell you the truth. If preachers loved their congregations, they would learn the truth and teach it to whoever attends the church service. Many of these poor excuses for preachers only have their best interest at heart, not the people who seem to hold on to their every word. God so loved the world that He gave His only begotten Son. (John 3:16) Jesus Christ loved us so much that He gave His life, dying a horrifying death on the cross. (Ephesians 5:1-2) Therefore be imitators of God as dear children. And walk in love, as Christ also has loved us and given Himself for us, an offering and a sacrifice to God for a sweet-swelling aroma."

Again, the question on the floor is, why is there a lack of love in the church? People hold a perception of God's love, and the church has fallen short of effectively conveying the true essence and meaning of God's love. "And we have known and believe the love that God has for us. God is love, and he who abides in love abides in God, and God in him." (1 John 4:16) The majority of churchgoers experience a lack of love because there is far too little abiding in God in their daily lives. If God is good all the time and all the time God is good, why is there so little time spent with Him? The word abide means to remain or stay around. Abiding is, "Hanging out with God." If we choose to hang around the Spirit of God consistently every day, God's love will rub off on us, because we are abiding. Abiding also brings obedience. The greatest commandment States, "Love the Lord your God with all your heart, with all your soul, and with all your strength. (Deuteronomy 6:5) Jesus took it a step further when He said, "Hear, O Israel, the Lord our God, the Lord is one. And you shall love the Lord your

God with all your heart, with all your soul, with all your mind, and with all your strength. This is the first commandment. And second is this: You shall love your neighbor as yourself. There is no other commandment greater than these." (Mark 12:29-31)

There is a false narrative that has been promoted in our society for decades. "The greatest love of all is to love yourself," is the theme song from the movie Ali. This is the opposite of what the Bible commands us to do. The world will always choose to differ from what the Bible says. There is nothing wrong with loving yourself, but it is not the greatest love of all. All of us were created in a unique way that is different than anyone else. The Bible says, "I will give thanks to You, for I am fearfully and wonderfully made; Wonderful are Your works, And my soul knows it very well." (Psalm 139:14) We must choose to believe what God says about us. Society paints a picture of not only what beauty is but also who we should love and what we should look like. We miss out on our blessings by having the wrong definition of love. Love requires sacrifice and giving of oneself. The church was created to bring a community of like-minded people together to not only glorify the Lord Jesus Christ on Sunday but throughout the week wherever we go or whatever we do.

God takes love very seriously, and we must. Loving people is very important to God regardless of how you feel. "If someone says, I love God, and hates his brother, he is a liar; for he who hates his brother whom he has seen; how can he love God whom he has not seen? And this commandment we have from Him: that he who loves God must love his brother also." (1 John 4:20-21) This is not just another verse in the Bible. Notice the importance of the word commandment in Mark 12:29-31 and 1 John 4:21. The greatest commandment, the first commandment, no other commandment, and this commandment, all point to obedience. We must learn the importance of obeying God all the time and not based on our feeling or how we feel especially when it comes to not only loving God but loving people. People are of the utmost importance to God because He sent His only begotten Son, Jesus Christ, to die for all the sins of the world so we could spend eternity with Him. Only for those who believe.

Many of us grapple with the challenge of acknowledging and embracing the belief in the only begotten Son of God. The manifestation of this struggle is often evident in our actions. Just witness the way we as churchgoers go about our daily lives. The evidence is very clear. When the Apostle Paul tells us to be imitators of God, he also warns us. "But fornicators and all uncleanness or covetousness, let it not even be named among you, as fitting for saints; neither filthiness, nor foolish talking, nor course jesting, which are not fitting, but rather giving thanks. For this, you know that no fornicator, unclean person, nor covetous man, who is an idolater, has any inheritance in the kingdom of God." (Ephesians 5:3-5)

Abiding or hanging out with God, gives us as believers the power to love people regardless of how we feel about that person. Love does not have anything to do with how you feel. Again, it is a commandment.

Additional evidence from the Bible can be found in 1 Corinthians chapter 13. In the Christian circles, it is known as the love chapter. If you read it and study it, it will reveal that love has nothing to do with feelings but everything to do with service. "Love suffers long and is kind; love does not envy; love does not parade itself, is not puffed up; does not behave rudely, does not seek its own, is not provoked, thinks no evil; does not rejoices in iniquity, but rejoices in truth; bears all things, hopes all things, endures all things. Love never fails." (1 Corinthians 13:4-8a) Wow, what a definition of love. Love has everything to do with the actions we take and the decisions we make when it comes to our relationships with others. Not just our relationships with other church members but people outside the church. I can testify that the reason why I can testify as to why I had some success in my marriage is because while we were married, I refused to let my wife take on more responsibilities in the home than me. Regardless of how I felt, there were some responsibilities in the home that she did not have to concern herself with. Was she incapable of performing some of those domestic duties? Of course not. But one of the ways to prove my love for God, was to wash the dishes, mop the floors, clean the bathrooms, vacuum the carpet, dust, and even cook. My love for her had nothing to do with how I felt about her, for me it was about being consistence and not putting those responsibilities on her. Because I love God and I wanted Him to know that I was willing to do all I could to make my marriage work. Did we have a perfect marriage? Of course not. Was it a good marriage? It was until another head popped up. When you have two heads in a marriage, it is not a marriage anymore but a two-headed monster. Unfortunately, after 24 years of marriage, we decided to get a divorce. One of the saddest days in my life, but a great opportunity to take my faith and trust in God to a new level. Just a side note. If the person you think you want to marry does not love the Lord Jesus Christ, then you should not marry them. It is impossible to truly love someone if you or they do not love Jesus.

People are drawn to Jesus by the way we love them and others. Jesus not only expressed but demonstrated His love for the world by dying on the cross. How did He feel about going to the cross? In the gospel of Luke Jesus is speaking to the Father, saying, "Father, if it is Your will, take this cup away from Me; nevertheless, not My will but Yours, be done. Then an angel appeared to Him from heaven, strengthening Him. And being in agony, He prayed more earnestly. Then His sweat became like great drops of blood falling down to the ground." (Luke 22:42-44) The love Jesus expressed to the world, His death on the cross to save the world from the wrath to come, to offer the world a way out of hell, to reconcile a world to the God of heaven had nothing to do with how He felt. He was born to die, and He agonized to the point of sweating blood. None of us can truly fathom the depth of emotions that Jesus experienced before openly showing His love for this fallen world. The Bible says, "For God so loved the world that He gave His only begotten Son. It didn't have anything to do with how Jesus felt, and it doesn't have anything to do with how we feel. Love is demonstrated through our actions. We must be nice to others and treat them with respect. Don't be puffed up or think more highly of yourself than you ought to. There is nothing more irritating than to be around someone who thinks they are all that.

People are appointed the so-called important positions in the church and get beside themselves. They are deceiving themselves and a handful of others with the illusion that they possess exceptional qualities or importance. It's as if they have entered an imaginary "shekinah glory" when they stand before others. A legend in their own mind. Working their way into heaven, which is impossible to do.

If you love God, you will do all you can to please Him. If you want to please God, love Him and allow Him to love people through you. What I'm saying is not an easy task. But if you pray and ask God to help you, He will. Also, the more you practice loving people the better you will get at it. Will they make you mad? Yes. Will they make you want to cuss? Yes, they will. Will disputes take place? Yes, but less and less frequently. Will they disappoint you? Yes, from time to time. Will some of them continue to be professional fault-finders? Yes, some things never change. None of these actions on the part of others gives us an excuse for not loving them. Always remember love has nothing to do with how you feel about someone, it has everything to do with how you treat them.

All of us are the same when it comes to how God feels about us. God so loved the world, that He gave us Jesus. But God does not see us all the same. True believers in the eyes of God are seen through the blood of Jesus. Whereas people who choose not to become believers or followers of Jesus Christ are sons of disobedience. The Bible even says they are children of the devil because they practice habitual sin as his spirit works through them, which results in the wrath of God coming upon them. Do you not realize that God sent Jesus on a rescue mission? Ephesians 2:1-2, And you, He made alive, who were dead in trespasses and sin, in which you once walked according to the course of this world, according to the prince of the power of the air, the spirit who now works in the sons of disobedience.

"For the eyes of the Lord are upon the righteous, and His ears are open to their prayers; but the face of the Lord is against those who do evil. (1 Peter 3:12)

We as believers are held to a different standard. The God of love expects more out of His children than the average person, even the average Christian/churchgoer. God not only expects us to love, but He is so gracious that He, and only He, gives us the power to love. So, what must we do as followers of Jesus to please His Father? It's summed up in Romans 12:9-13. "Let love be without hypocrisy. Abhor what is evil. Cling to what is good. Be kindly affectionate to one another with brotherly love, in honor giving preference to one another; not lagging diligence, fervent in the spirit, serving the Lord; rejoicing in hope, patient in tribulation, continuing steadfastly in prayer; distributing to the needs of the saints, given to hospitality." When we willingly choose to follow the teachings of the Lord Jesus Christ, we embrace a responsibility: the obligation to express love toward others. Will the devil and his children make it easy for us? Not at all. The good news is God has placed in us the power to love, so we can reap the benefits that come with being obedient.

There is so much hate on display in and outside the walls of the church. Has there ever been a time in our society where people constantly assault one another physically and verbally as much as they do now? There is no fear of the consequences of sowing bad seeds. Not only do people often lack love for both God and others, but there also appears to be a noticeable absence of reverence and fear toward God. "God demonstrates His own love toward us, in that why we were still sinners, Christ died for us." Romans 5:8

I cannot even start to explain the love God has for us. A person can only start to comprehend God's love by coming to the cross. Seeing yourself hanging there ready to be crucified. Then the Lord Jesus Christ appears and firmly declares that He will not let that happen. Take them down. It doesn't matter what they are guilty of. Crucify Me. I will take the punishment. Drive the nails through My hands, through my feet, but don't lay a hand on them. That is the love that a person needs to witness. It only comes through a broken spirit. When you shift your focus from yourself to Jesus, that's when salvation happens. By looking to Him, we find our way to salvation. He is the perfect example for us to follow. God took His Son, who knew no sin to be sin for us. Jesus Christ was not a sinner, but God treated Him as if He were, so you and I could have an opportunity to experience eternal life with the God of heaven. But only if we make the decision to do that.

Therefore, the Holy Spirit Says: "Today, if you hear His voice, Do not harden your hearts as in the rebellion, In the day of trail in the wilderness, Where your fathers tested Me, tried Me, And saw My works forty years. Therefore, I was angry with that generation, And Said, They always go astray in their hearts, And they have not known My ways. So, I swore by My wrath, They shall not enter my rest." Hebrews 3:7-11

The dangers of doubting and the dangers of disbelieving the promises of God point to the heart of individuals who choose to follow their owns ways, and chase after the gods of this world. There is a lack of love in the church because there is a lack of love for God. It is not God's will that we disobey His commandments. God's will is that we repent of our sins and develop a desire to know Him through His Son, Jesus Christ. You can't love this wicked world and the God of heaven at the same time. You will find yourself moving backward spiritually or like the Israelites, wandering in the wilderness for the rest of your life and never experiencing the promises of God.

Don't be hindered by the love that this world offers. It is not genuine love. The definition of worldly love leads a person down a road of disappointment, disbelief, and disaster. God's love is for those who have repented of their sins and believe the gospel.

Lack of Holiness

Why is there a lack of holiness in the church? Revelation chapter 2:9, and Revelation 3:9, refer to some churches as the "synagogue of Satan." Just because the name church is on a building or a building is built to look like a church, it does not mean that the actions or events taking place in that building are pleasing to God. In Matthew 16:13-14 Jesus asked His disciples a very important question. "Who do men say that I am? They answered and said, "Some say John the Baptist, some Elijah, and others Jeremiah or one of the prophets." Jesus then makes it personal and says in verse 15, "Who do you say that I am?" Peter steps up in verse 16 and says, "You are the Christ, the Son of the living God." Jesus, being pleased with the response, said to him, "Bless are you Simon Bar-Jonah, for flesh and blood has not revealed this to you, but my Father who is in heaven. And I also say to you that you are Peter, and on this rock, I will build My church, and the gates of hell shall not prevail against it."

The foundation of any church must be built on Jesus, the Son of God. He must be honored, worshiped, and adored. Jesus came to this earth to set a standard on how to have a relationship with God which means a life of holiness. Righteous living is an ingredient placed in the life of every Christian who truly believes that Jesus Christ is the Son of God. We must also believe that He is who He says he is, and that He is who the Bible says He is. He is God and we are not. Despite what some might tell you from the pulpit, stating, "We are little gods." We are not little gods. Children of God? Yes; those of us who have experienced the new birth.

When a person experiences a new birth, or what the Bible calls in John 3:3 "born again" the Holy Spirit comes to live on the inside of that believer. Therefore, a standard is placed in that believer's mind and on their heart to live holy. Becoming more and more like Jesus calls for a lifestyle of worship and holy living. For some of us, it's instantaneous. For me, it was a process.

When I first heard the gospel, I just happened to be in the right place at the right time. January 1995, I heard a message on the Holy Spirit. I did not get saved that day, but it drew my interest to the Bible, and the sermon gave me a desire to hear more. One morning alone at my sister's kitchen table I was reading 1 John chapter 1 and the Bible came alive to me. I saw in those first verses who Jesus was and who He is. I also realized who I was, a sinner who needed a Savior. After the light came on and realizing what a rotten sinner I was, tears started to flow. The question I needed an answer to; was why God would become a man and place Himself on a cross and die a horrific death for someone like me. A liar, a thief, a fornicator, a beer drinker, a weed smoker, an adulterer, an idol worshiper, and so much more. Once I found the answer it caused me to love and appreciate life like never before. The answer was in a verse that most of us who attend church memorize as children in Sunday school. John 3:16, "For God so loved the world that He gave His only begotten Son, that whoever believes in Him shall not perish, but have everlasting life." It was the first time I realized the power in that verse. God loved me, and He will never stop loving someone like me. I don't deserve it, I didn't earn it, I couldn't afford it, just had to believe it. God said it and the matter is settled. I am that person who deserved to be on the cross. But Jesus my Lord and Savior took my place. What a mighty God we serve.

I had to make some serious decisions about where I go from here. I looked at my past and I did not like or appreciate the sin. I discovered that I had to deal with the sin issue. The more I read, I discovered how much God hates sin. My new pleasure was to please God. I decide to follow Jesus. This was something new and exciting, and following Jesus made me not only feel better about myself, but it also made me feel better about life. So, when I ran across 1 Peter 1: 13-16 it helped point my mind in the right direction.

"Therefore gird up the loins of your mind, be sober, and rest your hope fully on the grace that is to be brought to you at the revelation of Jesus Christ; as obedient children, not conforming yourselves to the former lust, as in your ignorance; but as He who called you is holy, you also be holy in all your conduct, because it is written, "Be holy for I am holy." Notice it does not say to be holy in some of your conduct but be holy in all your conduct. God is a holy God and Peter is not asking us to be holy. He is pointing us in the right direction spiritually. He is telling us to take control. Don't allow an unholy lifestyle that you once lived to disobey what is written in Scripture. Don't allow ignorance to draw you back to a lifestyle of lust. Rest your hope. Enjoy the grace that is freely given. The revelation of Jesus, realizing who He really is, and what He did for you on the cross is a moment in time to be embraced by a new believer.

For the {remarkable undeserved} grace of God that brings salvation has appeared to all men. It teaches us to reject ungodliness and worldly (immoral) desires, and to live sensible, upright, and godly lives {lives with a purpose that reflect spiritual maturity} in this present age, awaiting and confidently expecting the {fulfillment of our} blessed hope and glorious appearing of our great God and Savior, Christ Jesus, who {willingly} gave Himself {to be crucified} on our behalf to redeem us and purchase our freedom from all wickedness, and to purify for Himself a chosen and very special people to be His own possession, who are enthusiastic for doing what is good. Titus 2:11-14 AMP

Jesus went to the cross so that believers could be made righteous in God's sight. When God looks at those of us who believe in the work that was done on the cross, He sees us through the blood of Jesus. His sacrifice made those who believed righteous, not holy. That's why 1 Peter says, "Gird up the loins of your mind." In other words, you must guard your mind. Your thoughts against all that you were formally involved in would keep you away from this wonderful revelation of discovering who Jesus Christ is.

Because revelation brings illumination which causes you to love Him and gives you a desire to please Him with godly conduct. Why, because it has been revealed to you who He really is. Jesus is not a prophet, meth, or just a name thrown around and misused on Sunday in most churches across this country. He is God. And right now, He is seated at the right hand of His Father. He is divine and He always will be divine. He was with God in the beginning, He was God and man when he walked on the earth, and He will be God when He returns. That is why Peter tells us to "Rest your hope fully on the grace that is to be brought to you at the revelation of Jesus Christ." Have expectations that are tied to spiritual success. Perform at a high level spiritually, as you develop a desire to live for Jesus Christ and walk in the ways of righteousness.

Once I received more and more revelation, I decided that I wanted to please God. The first thing I had to do was take my Bible and commit spiritual suicide. I could not allow my flesh to get in the way of my spiritual success. I was and I still am in a battle that I'm determined to win. My flesh and its desires did not want to let go of the investment and the time it had put into making me who I was, a rotten sinner. But I ran across more revelation. "For we do not commend ourselves again to you, but give you an opportunity to boast on our behalf, that you may have an answer to those who boast in appearance and not in heart. For if we are beside ourselves, it is for God; or if we are of sound mind, it is for you. For the love of Christ compels us, because we judge thus: that if One died for all, then all died; and He died for all, that those who live should no longer live for themselves, but for Him who died for them and rose again. Therefore, from now on we regard no one according to the flesh. Even though we have known Christ according to the flesh, yet now we know Him thus no longer. Therefore, if anyone is in Christ, he is a new creation, old things have passed away; behold all things have become new." (1 Corinthians 5:12-17) That meant to me that spiritual suicide was the right thing to do at that point in my life.

Kill the flesh and its lustful thoughts. I was excited about the new me, and where my Lord would take me. It was the best decision I had ever made. My life and my lifestyle became a witness to the miracle-working power of the gospel of Jesus Christ. God is still in the miracle-working business.

Some of the greatest miracles being done by God today are changing the lives and spiritual direction of an individual life. A person accepting Jesus Christ as not only their Savior but deciding to make Him the Lord of their life is a spiritual miracle. For repentance to take place, and a decision to be made to live your life as a follower of Jesus, that is the miracle-working power of the gospel.

Lack of Peace

Why is there a lack of peace in the church? There is not only a lack of peace in the church but also a lack of peace in the lives of many people who attend church. "Peace I leave with you; My peace I give to you; not as the world gives, do I give you." (John 14:27) We as Christians have allowed the world to define peace for our everyday way of life instead of hearing and knowing what our Bible says about peace. Instead of the peace the Bible offers, we look for and want the piece that is promoted by this world system. The world defines peace as a material piece instead of the peace Jesus is speaking about in John. The church has allowed that same philosophy in some of the pulpits of our churches, and it results in members looking for a piece instead of the peace of God. The world offers a piece that you can see, touch, and sometimes smell. But God offers a peace that surpasses all understanding.

There are a lot of words in our vocabulary that sound the same, but their definitions are different. The word peace/piece is no exception. They both can bring satisfaction, but the end results are temporal vs eternal. It was amazing to me that when I looked in the dictionary at the word temporal, of course, it meant temporary, but it also meant material possessions, esp. ecclesiastical revenues. As opposed to eternal which has no beginning or end in relation to time.

Before I was redeemed and washed in the blood of the Lamb of God, I also focused on the piece instead of peace. It was more important for me to have a car, cloths, a place to stay, a girlfriend, a party, or a nightclub just to name a few things. The peace that is offered by the Lord Jesus Christ was a mystery to me simply because of my lack of knowledge. I allowed the things of this world to become pleasure which always ends up having no lasting value. The peace I've experienced knowing the Lord Jesus Christ is a never-ending peace. A day-in-day-out peace that cannot be explained, only experienced. If I was forced to explain or put a title on this peace, I would call it a "loving peace." Knowing how much God loves me and wants to reward me for my obedience to His Word sums up my peace that surpasses understanding.

The Bible tells us in Matthew 6:33 "But seek first the kingdom of God and His righteousness, and all these things shall be added to you." God knows what you need. He is all-knowing, and He promises to supply all your needs according the His riches and glory. But He requires that we seek Him first and His righteousness. Once you decide to seek Him you will discover that He is righteous, holy, and just. In the same chapter verse 24, Jesus says, "No one can serve two masters; for either you will hate the one and love the other, or else he will be loyal to one and despise the other. You can't serve God and mammon." Then in verses 25-34, He gives us instructions on how to conquer the number one weapon used by the devil to destroy our peace, and that weapon is worry. "Therefore, I say to you, do not worry about your life." (Matthew 6:25a) To worry is to feel undue care or anxiety; mental disturbance due to care and anxiety. When a person seeks piece instead of peace, the cares of this world steal the peace that only comes when our number one focus is the God of this universe. The Bible says that He will keep you in perfect peace if your mind stays on Him. (Isaiah 26:3). What does it mean to keep your mind on God? When your mind stays on God, it means that your mind stays on high alert to do that which pleases God. When we are obedient to the word of God, He gives us the conformation we as believers need so that we can continue to practice righteousness which leads to the peace that surpasses all understanding as we continue to grow in the faith. "Rejoice in the Lord always. Again, I will say, rejoice! Let your gentleness be known to all men. The Lord is at hand. Be anxious for nothing, but by prayer and supplication, with thanksgiving let your request be known to God; and the peace of God which surpasses all understanding, will guard your hearts and minds through Christ Jesus." (Phil. 4:4-7)

How can the Lord be there to help if your mind is not on Him? In order to act or react to every situation that arises, you must program your mind to stay on high spiritual alert. We must continue to practice the spiritual wisdom that has freely been given to us by using the instructions that are written in the Bible to have success. It is even more important to believe what is written so you can act or react with confidence in God and not yourself. The Bible tells us to have no confidence in the flesh. (Phil. 3:3) It will fail you every time. Most times we might think we know how to handle a certain situation or even make good decisions, and sometimes we do. The question on the floor is it the right decision? In Proverbs 1:2-5 King Solomon writes, "To know wisdom and instruction, to perceive the words of understanding, to receive the instruction of wisdom, Justice, judgment, equity; to give prudence to the simple, to the young man knowledge and discretion. A wise man hears and increases learning, and a man of understanding will attain wise counsel."

I will attempt to define 3 words written in that passage. Equity is fairness; equal adjustment or distribution; giving to each his due according to the sense of natural right. In other words, be fair, play fair, and act and be fair-minded when it comes to making decisions in every area of life.

Webster writes that prudence or to be prudent means cautious and judicious; careful; not extravagant. We must take this wisdom that God has made available to us and move with caution and wisdom. And at the same time understand that it is His advice and not yours alone or the advice of others that you are basing your decision on. Sometimes we are tempted to seek the advice of people and there isn't anything wrong with that if we seek wise godly advice.

I'd also would like to talk about the word discretion. Webster tells us it's the quality of being discreet; prudence; discernment; and liberty to act according to one's judgment. John MacArthur writes, "to make one ponder before sinning, thus, to make a responsible choice." Discretion/discernment if used properly is a power tool. When you use a power tool the energy coming from it saves you a lot of time and saves you from the trouble of doing it manually using your own strength. When you use discretion, you are substituting godly wisdom which can save you a lot of time and energy if you had not used it. If we as a nation had used just a little discretion in pass elections both locally and especially in our national elections, there is a great chance we would be experiencing better times in our country. Discretion leads to peace of mind because you feel better about the godly decision you've made.

When we allow anything to dominate our thoughts other than the Spirit of God, there is a much greater chance that it will lead to worry or anxiety. Which can and has become a health issue for many people who attend church. This ought not to be the case. The Bible is a tool that defeats worry and anxiety every time. People carry the cares of this world on their shoulders which can be heavy and weighty which causes them to become spiritual hunchbacks. Even though they appear to be walking in an upright position, spiritually their upper body is at a 45-degree angle, because they have not learned to rid themselves of those cares.

But I have good news for all who need to hear. We have a Savior who is near and wants to take on that weigh only because He cares. We must be willing to take the steps necessary to get Him involved. 1 Peter 5:7 says, "Therefore humble yourselves under the mighty hand of God, that He may exalt you in due time, casting all your cares upon Him because He cares for you." Now we must look carefully at the next verse because there are consequences for not learning how to cast all your cares on Jesus Christ. Verse 8 says "Be sober, be vigilant, because your adversary the devil walks around like a roaring lion seeking whom he may devour." Do you not know that the devil is behind all our anxieties and problems that cause us to worry? He is the author of confusion, and his desire is to destroy all of us. We must stay alert and put our confidence in Jesus our Lord who is willing to take on all situations that can sometimes come out of nowhere.

"Peace I leave with you, My peace I give to you; not as the world gives do I give to you. Let not your heart be troubled, neither let it be afraid." (John 14:27) This peace Jesus is speaking of is the peace that truly surpasses understanding. Regardless of your situation this peace substance you. There may be turmoil all around, but you don't have to be shaken by it because of this peace. There is so much going on in our day-in and day-out lives. So, Jesus is telling us that regardless of what is going on you can choose the peace of God. When you choose peace, you become steadfast and unmovable in your everyday way of life. Of course, that everyday way of life must include a walk with Jesus and being obedient to His word. This peace only comes when we make up our minds to keep His commandments. Obedience not only gives you peace, but it proves your love for Him. John 14:15 & 21 "If you love Me keep my commandments" "He who has My commandments and keeps them, it is he who loves Me. And he who loves Me will be loved by My Father, and I will love him and manifest Myself to him." The more you come to know Jesus as He manifests Himself to you, the more peace you have because He is the Prince of peace.

Lack of Teaching

There is a lack of what is most important in a church service today, and that is a lack of teaching. "How then shall they call on Him in whom they have not believed? And how shall they believe on Him of whom they have not heard? And how shall they hear without a preacher? And how shall they preach unless they are sent? As it is written: How beautiful are the feet of those who preach the gospel of peace, who bring glad tidings of good things!" (Romans 10:14-15)

You hear preachers or so-called Reverends stating that they were called. Called by who? We are all called to live a life of obedience. The life we live must paint a picture that attracts unbelievers to someone who is different spiritually. The problem is they were not called to preach but they are like all true believers, are called to be conformed to the image of God's Son the Lord Jesus Christ. (Romans 8:29)

Paul writes in 1 Timothy 3:1, This is a faithful saying: If a man desires the position of a bishop, he desires a good work. He does not say if a man is called to be a bishop. In Titus 1:5, Paul instructed Titus to appoint elders in every city in Crete.

In 1 Timothy 3:2-7, he then goes on the explain the qualifications of a church leader. A bishop then must be blameless, the husband of one wife, temperate, sober-minded, of good behavior, hospitable, able to teach, not given to wine, not violent, not greedy for money, but gentle, not quarrelsome, not covetous; one who rules his own house well, having his children in submission with all reverence, (for if a man does not know how to rule his own house, how can he take care of the church of God?); not a novice, lest being puffed up with pride he fall into the same condemnation as the devil. Moreover, he must have a good testimony among those who are outside, lest he fall into reproach and the snare of the devil.

Most of these men and women in the pulpits are bought and paid for by this antichrist 501(c)(3) system. A non-profit organization that allows federal tax exemption for organized churches and other non-profit organizations, and it is run by the IRS. This system has been used by the church organization to set up businesses so that most of the money made never goes to those who need it most. Instead, people are robbed of their hard-earned money because the mindset of a greedy person is that enough is never enough. They manipulate the hearts and minds of those who attend and lack discernment through the teaching of the false doctrine of tithing. When men and women preachers are involved in a church for any reason other than to save the soul of other men or women, they are instruments used by satan to preach a gospel of manipulation instead of the gospel of Jesus Christ. They stand in those pulpits Sunday after Sunday lying as they are determined to run a successful business, not a church. The more successful the business the more entertainment intensifies. More flesh on display and less Holy Ghost power on display. People's lives are not being changed through the preaching of the gospel of Jesus Christ. Instead, they listen intently to Rev, bishop, pastor, or Dr. so and so says. Remember God works all things out for those who love Him because He predestined us to be conformed to the image of His dear Son, Jesus Christ.

Most of these preachers aren't conformed because most of these preachers don't know Jesus. They know of Jesus, and they use His name to take total advantage of so many members who have not come into the knowledge of who Jesus Christ is. That's why they can get away with telling the lie they have been called to preach. So, when you lack discernment and you have very little to no knowledge of the scriptures, you are deceived by what comes out of the mouths of people who have an agenda that does not line up with the definition of what a church looks like. Again, these people are not called, they develop and desire these positions.

"I, therefore, the prisoner of the Lord, beseech you to walk worthy of the calling with which you were called, with all lowliness and gentleness, with longsuffering, bearing with one another in love, endeavoring to keep unity of the Spirit in the bond of peace. There is one body and one Spirit, just as you were called in the hope of your calling." (Eph. 4:1-4)

Why is there so much unnecessary confusion and tumult in many churches today, when we are called to walk worthy with all lowliness (humility) and gentleness, bearing or putting up with one another in love? That responsibility falls in the lap of ministers who stand up every Sunday and are given the opportunity to express to the congregation what the word of the Lord is saying. Instead, there is a lack of preparation on display that only a person with discernment and concern for the souls of those in attendance can pick up on, and there is very little "rightly dividing the word of truth." (2 Timothy 2:15)

Romans 8:28-29 says, "And we know that all things work together for the good of those who love God, to those who are called according to His purpose. For whom He foreknew, He also predestined to be conformed to the image of His Son, that we might be the firstborn among many brethren."

Preachers are not exempt from being conformed. It's God's purpose for all believers to be conformed to the image of Jesus Christ. That is why He predestined us. All Christians are called. We are called to put away the old way of living and to put on Christ and learn His characteristics. Many who stand before congregations Sunday after Sunday fail to meet the criteria of what the Bible defines as a good minister of Jesus Christ. Nourished in the word of faith and good doctrine which we must carefully follow. (1 Timothy 4:6) Men not women are required to be committed to not only the teaching of God's word but also to live out the truth of Scripture. People who come to hear you preach Sunday after Sunday, need to know that what you are teaching them, is being lived out by the person who is doing the teaching. Far too many shepherds fail in the area of being an example to the flock. Which allows the flock to fail miserably at being an example of those who don't attend church. Failing in the area to display what a godly life looks like is a 'mestiomy,' not a testimony of the power of the gospel. Therefore, those who aren't members of a church don't attend because of the inappropriate spiritual behavior that is displayed by most church members.

Romans 1:7 and 1 Corinthians 1:3, Paul is writing to Christians, to those who are sanctified in Jesus Christ, called to be saints. We are called to be set apart from sin which so easily ensnares us. (Hebrew 12:1) We are called to be different from the people who aren't saints. From people who love this world and the things of this world. "Do not love the world and the things in the world. If anyone loved the world, the love of the Father is not in him. For all that is in the world—the lust of the flesh, the lust of the eyes, and the pride of life—is not of the Father but of the world." (1 John 2:15) Your affection must be for God and people. Christians, and non-Christians, not the world system.

"For you, brethren, have been called to liberty; (Galatians 5:13a) we are called to freedom in Christ Jesus. Freedom to worship our Lord and Savior Jesus Christ from the heart and not in a ritual, ceremonial, or by the tradition of those who were before us. Which does not allow the Holy Spirit to move and touch the hearts of unbelievers. "Beware lest anyone cheat you through philosophy and empty deceit, according to the tradition of men, according to the basic principles of the world, and not according to Christ. For in Him dwells all the fullness of the Godhead bodily; and you are complete in Him, who is the head of all principality and power." (Colossians 2:8-10) Rituals and traditions are put in place by men and they do not point us to the basics of the gospel truth, which is to love God and others. Liberty allows love to flow through the congregation. We must teach the truth of Scripture and allow the Holy Spirit to flow richly in our hearts and minds. If that does not take place, we are warned of the consequences. "For all the law is fulfilled in one word, even in this: You shall love your neighbor as yourself. But if you bite and devour one another, beware lest you be consumed by one another" (Gal. 5:14-15)

We are also called to peace and to be thankful. "And let the peace of God rule in your hearts, to which you were also called in one body to be thankful." (Colossians 3:15) When your life lines up with the gospel of Jesus Christ it teaches you to be thankful for the peace that it brings. Not only peace but the security of eternal life. You experience Colossians 3:16-17. "Let the word of Christ dwell in you richly in all wisdom, teaching and admonishing one another in psalms and hymns and spiritual songs, singing with grace in your hearts to the Lord. And whatever you do in word or deed, do all in the name of the Lord Jesus, giving thanks to God the Father through Him."

We are called to lay hold of eternal life as we concentrate on godliness in our daily walk with Jesus Christ. 1 Timothy 6:12. "Fight the good fight of faith, lay hold on eternal life, to which you were called and have confessed the good confession in the presence of many witnesses."

"But you are a chosen generation, a royal priesthood, a holy nation, His own special people, that you may proclaim the praises of Him who called you out of darkness into His marvelous light:" (1 Peter 2:9) Jesus Christ came to shine light on the truth of God's word.

I once was blind, but now I see are lyrics from the song amazing grace, sung in most church services every week. Most church members are truly blind to the realty of the risen Christ, and we must be delivered from the god of this world (the devil) who has been given the authority to keep people who don't believe in Jesus, in darkness. "But even if our gospel is veiled, it is veiled to those who are perishing, whose mind the god of this age has blinded, who do not believe, lest the light of the gospel of the glory of Christ, who is the image of God, should shine on them. (2 Corinthians 4:3-4)

It is so important for us as church members to examine Scripture for ourselves; to know and understand what is preached in our services every Sunday. "Let God be true and every man a liar" (Romans 3:4) Most of these preachers do very little studying of the Bible. That is proven by the words that come out of their mouths and the way services are conducted. Most of what is preached does not line up with Scripture, therefore no application takes place in the lives of church members. They leave emotionalized without instructions on how to achieve victory over the devil because of a lack of teaching coming from most pulpits.

Peter, in 1 Peter chapter 5 talks about shepherding or overseeing a flock or congregation. "Shepherd the flock of God, which is among you, serving as overseers, not by compulsion but willingly, not for dishonest gain but eagerly; nor as being lords over those entrusted to you, but being examples to the flock;" Why? Because "when the Chief Shepherd appears, you will receive the crown of glory that does not fade away."

(1 Peter 5:2-4)

Most ministers don't know about this crown of glory because they don't read and study the Bible. There are a lot of talented guys out there who don't play professional sports because they refuse to put the work in; and pay the price to perfect the craft. Being a preacher/pastor is going to call for a man to put the work in. Studying the Bible, reading related materials, spending time alone with God in prayer, and seeking the Holy Spirit for help and guidance in their everyday walk with Christ. There are so many distractions that can so easily pull a minister away from the time he needs to prepare to deliver divine truth. And if your motives are not lined up with God's purpose, which is to bring people to the knowledge of the truth, then you cannot fulfill the role of an overseer that Peter is writing about in 1 Peter chapter 5. Peter is telling the minister not to oversee a congregation because you feel it is something you must or have to do, but it should be done whole heartedly, with gladness, with joy, and knowing that this is an honor and a privilege God has given you. Pastors must realize that this is a special favor from the King of kings and the Lord of lords to stand before a congregation and teach the Word of God. You can't stand before people whom God Himself has placed in your presence at this time in history like it's a privilege for them to hear what you have to say. If you have spent quality time with God, they should be hearing from Him and not some nonsense you have to say.

There are several important points Peter makes in these verses. The first being the subject of serving. Jesus Christ set the ultimate example of being a servant. He just didn't talk the talk, but He walked the walk. "Whoever wants to become great among you must be your servant, and whoever wants to be first must be a slave. Just as the Son of Man did not come to be served, but to serve, and to give His life as a ransom for many." (Matthew 20:26-28) Jesus served us all the way to Calvary the place of Christ's crucifixion. I have seen pastors who can't even carry their owe Bible. They sit around desiring to be served instead of serving.

Then Peter tells them not to do it for money, he calls it dishonest gain. There is nothing wrong with a pastor/preacher getting paid or receiving a salary. The Bible tells us that "A laborer is worthy of his wages" (1 Timothy 5:18) but don't allow your motives or the reason why you pastor be only for getting money, being greedy for money, or loving money, the Bible warns against that. Instead, there should be an earnest desire to oversee the hearts and souls of the individuals who make the decision to attend the church you are affiliated with, if that is what you have really been called to do.

Another problem expressed by Peter is the dictatorship mentality. These people are entrusted to you so be careful how you treat them. You are not a master but an example of how to have success as a follower of the Lord Jesus Christ. Remember Ephesians 4 tells us to walk worthy of the calling which we are called. Don't live a defeated Christian life, unable to deal with the attacks of the evil one. But walk in victory with all humility willing to confess your sins to the Lord, for the Bible calls for all of us to confess.

Pastors are not superheroes. They must be held accountable and are accountable to God, who is keeping a record of all our actions. And there is no creature hidden from His sight, but all things are naked and open to the eyes of Him to whom we must give account. Hebrews 4:13 The congregation, the members of churches have a responsibility also. Hebrews 13:17 says, obey those who rule over you, and be submissive, for they watch out for your souls, as those who must give account. Let them do so with joy and not with grief, for that would be unprofitable for you.

A pastor should have a desire to receive that "crown of glory that does not fade away." Pastors need the Lord on their side, and He is not coming to help if you are not willing to develop that relationship with Him based on humility. We all need the grace (God's unmerited favor) of God, and it starts with humility.

1 Peter 5: 5b says, "And be clothed with humility for God resist the proud but gives grace to the humble." I have seen these proud and puffed-up spirits in pastors and preachers in many churches I have attended, and my discernment kicks in when I see it on television or hear it on the radio. Preachers exalting themselves as they mesmerized these congregations with fables and turned away from the truth of the Bible. (1 Timothy 1:4)

2 Timothy 4:1-4 instructs and warns pastors, "I charge you therefore before God and the Lord Jesus Christ, who will judge the living and the dead at His appearing and His kingdom: Preach the word! Be ready in season and

out of season. Convince, rebuke, exhort, with all longsuffering and teaching. For the time will come when they will not endure sound doctrine, but according to their own desires, because they have itching ear, they will heap up for themselves teachers: and they will turn their ears away from the truth and be turned aside to fables."

The evidence pointing to us as members of the churches today is that there are many members who do not endure sound doctrine, and we walk away from the truth of the Bible. And it sure does not help when truth is not being taught or practiced by the pastor.

We must take the Bible and what is written in it very seriously. And we must respect what is written in it. We must make up our minds to walk worthy of what we as pastors/preachers and saints are called to do. To present the word of God to the congregation after careful and intense study and allowing the Holy Spirit of God to take the stage and speak through us to the hearts and minds of those in attendance.

1 Timothy 4:16 says "Take heed to yourself and to doctrine. Continue in them, for in doing this you will save both yourself and those who hear you."

There is so much at stake when a man gets up and speaks to a group of people about what is written in the Bible. We must give full attention to the true doctrine of the gospel of Jesus Christ and stay with it because the bottom line is the people who are hearing you, need to be saved and those who are saved need a godly message that can be applied to the everyday issue of life.

I'm sure that this doesn't apply to most of you reading this because most of you have never consumed alcohol. Using alcohol is very dangerous for not only your body but it affects your mind and your spirit as well. Alcohol can impress on your mind to participate in some activities that if you weren't under the influence, you would have second thoughts about trying. It can make you sing when you know you can't, it will make you fight when you know you can't, and what is most dangerous about alcohol is that it tells your mind to continue to consume more of it when you know it can only lead to you becoming more and more like someone that you and others with you don't know.

Some preachers are like alcoholics, full of themselves. They try to sing when they know they can't, they make ungodly decisions that lead to fights and discord in the church, and the more they get consumed by themselves it makes them become more and more like the devil because they become puffed up and proud. The church they are in becomes their church and not the church of the living God. The congregation is robbed from hearing divine truth because you have someone under the influence of themselves, and not under the influence of the Holy Spirit of God, which leads to reckless indiscretion. God speaks through the prophet Jeremiah in Chapter 5:30-31. "An astonishing and horrible thing has been committed in the land; The prophets prophesy falsely, And the priest rule by their own power, And My people love to have it so. But what will you do in the end?"

When taking on the responsibility or position of a pastor you have an opportunity to be used to deliver the word of God to a congregation and to yourself because your soul is at stake along with the congregation. It is not an easy task, but it can be rewarding and beneficial. God loves a man after His own heart, but God also loves and cares about the people who come and listen to a man who has positioned himself to be used in a mighty way to bring a people to the true knowledge and understanding of who God is. If you're not under the influence of the Spirit of God, try humility, it works every time.

Lack of Wisdom

There is a lack of wisdom in the church. Webster defines wisdom as a quality of being wise; knowledge and the capacity to make use of it. Wisdom is the ability to apply knowledge and understanding. The Bible says, "Happy is the man who finds wisdom, And the man who gain understanding." (Proverbs 3:13) "The fear of the LORD is the beginning of wisdom, And knowledge of the Holy One is understanding. (Proverbs 9:10)

Wisdom speaks in Proverbs 8:32-36. "Now therefore listen to me, my children, For blessed are those who keep my ways. Hear instructions and be wise, And do not disdain it. Blessed is the man who listens to me, Watching daily at my gates, Waiting at the post of my doors. For whoever finds me finds life And obtains favor from the Lord. But he who sins against me wrongs his own soul; And those who hate me love death."

Most churches and most of its leaders have forsaken the wisdom of the Bible. Some have chosen to turn from the wisdom that the Bible offers, to the wisdom of man. There is a tremendous difference between what man teaches and what the Spirit of God teaches. Until a church becomes Spirit lead, most of its members cannot understand the things that the Spirit is teaching us in Scripture. The Bible teaches that a natural man is unable to understand Scripture. He is also unable to discern the things of this world that are going on all around him because all the treasures of wisdom and knowledge are hidden in the Father and in Christ. (Colossians 2:2-3) It is a mystery to him and foolishness to most church members and its leaders today. We would rather turn to man's wisdom or the wisdom of this world for answers to the everyday issues of life.

Wisdom calls aloud outside; She raises her voice in the open square, She cries out in the chief concourse, At the opening of the gates in the city she speaks her words: "How long you simple ones, will you love simplicity? For scorners delight in their scorning, And fools hate knowledge. Turn at my rebuke; Surely I will pour out my spirit on you; I will make my words known to you. Because you disdained all my counsel, And would have none of my rebuke, I also will laugh at your calamity; I will mock when your terror comes, When your terror comes like a storm, And your destruction like a whirlwind, When distress and anguish comes upon you. Then they will call upon me and I will not answer; They will seek me diligently, but they will not find me. Because they hated knowledge and did not choose the fear of the Lord." Proverbs 1:20-29

"To know wisdom and instruction, to perceive the words of understanding. To receive the instruction of wisdom, justice, judgement, and equity; to give prudence to the simple, to the young man knowledge and discretion. A wise man will hear and increase learning and a man of understanding will attain wise counsel." (Proverbs 1:2-5)

These verses point to the importance of wisdom, knowledge, understanding, and discretion. The Holy Spirit not only makes wisdom available for us but as He fills us with this knowledge, He gives us the ability to understand and discern what we hear, see, and learn. You can obtain all the knowledge in the world, but if you don't understand what you have obtained, that knowledge can't work for you. People who attend church know that there is a God. Some even know that there is a God, and He has a Son named Jesus. But if you don't understand why there is a God and why He had a Son, then just having knowledge of God will not do you any good.

Along with knowledge comes wisdom and understanding. That is why the Apostle Paul prayed in Ephesians 1:17-19 "That the God of our Lord Jesus Christ, the Father of glory, may give to you the spirit of wisdom and revelation in the knowledge of Him, the eyes of your understanding being enlightened; that you know what is the hope of His calling, what are the riches of the glory of His inheritance in the saints, and what is the exceeding greatness of His power toward us who believe, according to the working of His mighty power." We must not only know and understand that Jesus came to earth to save us from our sins, but it is more important that we believe it. In verse 19, the Apostle Paul writes about this exceeding power toward us who believe. We must know and believe that Christ Jesus is not only the Son of God who humbled Himself, but that Jesus is God, and He is alive, and He is right now seated at God's right hand until that appointed time of His return to this earth. That we continue to live out and promote God's plan of salvation for those who believe and those who do not believe. We must know and believe that God the Father, needed a perfect sacrifice to save the world from the wrath to come. Romans 3:23 says, "For all have sinned and fall short of the glory of God." Every human is born into sin and all of us carry a sinful nature and until we experience the new birth, we are spiritually dead.

Far more than anything else, a spiritually dead person needs to be made alive by God. Salvation brings spiritual life to a spiritually dead person. So, what is a spiritually dead person? A spiritually dead person is anyone who does not have a serious relationship with God the Father through our Lord Jesus Christ. We as human beings are born that way. You don't come into this world loving anybody or anything but yourself. That is why Jesus said in John 3:3 "that you must be born again. It is a spiritual awaking. You are made alive by God Himself to the reality of what life is all about. Life is about three things; 1. Praising the name of Jesus; 2. Living holy; 3. Giving God the credit for everything going on in your life. You not only must praise Him when everything is going well, but you learn to praise Him in difficult times as well. (Keep in mind that your situation could be worse.)

We love God when everything seems to be going our way, but we have questions and develop doubts about God when problems arise, and unexpected circumstances hit us at a time when wc least expect it. The problem with most of us is that we look to people for answers to the circumstances first and we choose to seek God through prayer or seek godly wisdom that could start to point us in the right direction last. We make the mistake of thinking that most people we know want to help us. When in all actuality they don't. The Bible says we are cursed when we put our trust in man, and we are blessed when we trust in the LORD. (Jeremiah 17:5&7)

Jeremiah 17:9-10 says, "The heart is deceitful above all things, and desperately wicked; who can know it.? I, the LORD, search the heart, I test the mind, even to give every man according to his ways, according to the fruit of his doing."

God's desire is to change our hearts, to change our minds, our way of thinking. He wants us to pray like David prayed in Psalm 51:10 "Create in me a clean heart, O God, And renew a steadfast spirit within me."

We all need a new heart or a clean heart that comes with a new spirit because before we come to know the Father of our Lord and Savior Jesus Christ, our understand of God has been darkened by ungodly spirits. We don't even have a desire to know the true and living God. We just go to church on Sunday from 11-1 and get a little taste of God and struggle Sunday afternoon, as soon as we walk out the door of the church, until the next Sunday morning at 11:00, because in most cases we are not receiving any information on how to win spiritually inside or outside the walls of the church. Ephesians 4:17-18 tells us "That you should no longer walk as the rest of the Gentiles walk, in the futility of their mind, having their understanding darkened, being alienated from the life of God, because of the ignorance that is in them, because of the blindness of their heart."

John MacArthur writes in his commentary about the futility of the mind. "First, unbelievers are intellectually unproductive. As far as spiritual and moral issues are concerned, their rational processors are distorted and inadequate, inevitably failing to produce godly understanding or moral living. Their life is empty, vain, and without meaning."

That is why in Ezekiel 36:26-27 God says, "I will give you a new heart and put a new spirit within you; I will take the heart of stone out of your flesh and give you a heart of flesh. I will put My Spirit within you and cause you to walk in My statutes, and you will keep My judgments and do them."

How can any of us walk in God's statutes, keep His judgments, or do them if we lack godly wisdom? We may be successful or obtain wisdom in a career, or specialize in a profession, but worldly wisdom will only take us so far. We must be careful to not become wise in our own minds. The Bible warns against that. It is easy to develop a lack of thanksgiving and a mindset that we don't need the Lord to help us achieve this temporary success. Trust in the lord with all your heart And lean not on your own understanding; In all your ways acknowledge Him, And He shall direct your paths. Do not be wise in your own eyes; Fear the Lord and depart from evil. Proverbs 3:5-7 Believers are not to be conceited or develop a feeling of superiority.

We must develop a desire to gain wisdom knowledge and understanding of how to gain spiritual success before we are able to gain success in other areas of our lives. Peter tells us in 1 Peter 4:3 "For we have spent enough of our past lifetime in doing the will of the Gentiles-when we walked in lewdness, lust, drunkenness, revelries, drinking parties, and abominable idolatries." I like The Living Bible version. You have had enough in the past of the evil things the godless enjoy—sex sin, lust, getting drunk, wild parties, drinking bouts, and the worship of idols, and other terrible sins.

God's desire is to deliver every one of us out of this ungodly system that is set up to destroy us. It set all of us up for a great fall. Gaining wisdom, knowledge, and understanding is vitally important as we look at what the author of Proverb writes. Chapter 2:5 "For the Lord gives wisdom; From His mouth come knowledge and understanding." Verses 10-12, "When wisdom enters your heart, And knowledge is pleasant to your soul, Discretion will preserve you; Understanding will keep you, To deliver you from the way of evil, From the man who speaks perverse things." Chapter 3:13, "Happy is the man who finds wisdom, And the man who gains understanding; Verses 19-20 "The Lord by wisdom founded the earth; By understanding He established the heavens; By His knowledge the depths were broken up, And the clouds drop down the dew." Chapter 4:5a "Get wisdom! Get understanding! Verse 7-8 "Wisdom is the principal thing; Therefore, get wisdom. And in all your getting, get understanding. Exalt her, and she will promote you; She will bring you honor, when you embrace her." Chapter 7:4 "Say to wisdom, "You are my sister," And call understanding your nearest kin,"

The key to having spiritual success in our churches is to gain all the wisdom, all the knowledge, and all the understanding we can about the Word of God. The message of Jesus Christ dying on the cross is foolishness to the world, to those who are perishing and on their way to hell. But to the church, to those who attend and are being saved, it is the power of God. (1 Corinthians 1:18) Our hearts and our way of thinking are vital to our victory in life. We find ourselves in unfortunate situations because of a lack of wisdom. Jesus not only came to save us from our sins, but He also came so that we might have life and have it more abundantly. (John 10:10)

This life we live has been designed by God, the creator of life, for us to enjoy. The key is obtaining the wisdom, that is throughout the Scriptures and applying the knowledge, then activating the understanding. If we can decide to grasp wisdom, knowledge, and understanding of the temporal, surely if we desire to, we can do it when it comes to the subject of eternity.

Once we understand the importance of eternity, we become like the apostle Paul in Romans 10;1 when he writes, "Brethren, my heart's desire and prayer, to God for Israel is that they be saved." Paul understood that people knew there was a God, but like a lot of church members today they weren't saved. Jesus walked among the Hebrews and preformed miracles and most of them still did not believe in Him. In Mark 16:14, Jesus reprimanded His disciples for their unbelief after He told them He would be killed and rise again. "Later He appeared to the eleven as they sat at the table; and He rebuked their unbelief and hardness of heart, because they did not believe those who had seen Him after He had risen." Jesus is preforming miracles today and there are a lot of us who don't believe in Him. So, you ask how is Jesus performing miracles today? When an old wretched sinner like me can hear the gospel of Jesus Christ, repent, and turn from his wicked ways, that's a miracle.

To gain wisdom, knowledge, and understanding of the truth of God's word is a miracle. There are people who attend church all their lives, some several times a week, and still don't come to understand the truth of Scripture. There are those who not only attend every Sunday and several times a week all their lives but there are also some who sit under great teaching of Scripture and still lack understanding and application of the word of God. That is why Paul writes in Romans 10:2 "They have a zeal for God, but not according to knowledge." He continues in verses 3 & 4 with a powerful observation, "For they being ignorant of God's righteousness, and seeking to establish their own righteousness, have not submitted to the righteousness of God. For Christ is the end of the law for righteousness to everyone who believes."

Most people who attend church never come to a full understanding of what it means to be obedient to God and to live a righteous life. According to Scripture, "all of our righteous are like filthy rags" (Isaiah 64:6) Unfortunately, there is a self-righteous spirit that has infiltrated the hearts and minds of many churchgoers, because they have not discovered justification. The fact that we are made righteous only because of what Jesus Christ did for us on the cross.

Do you know how the Bible describes a person who refuses to obtain the wisdom, knowledge, and understanding of what is written in the Bible? They are called fools. (Psalm 14:1 & 53:1) Deciding to submit to the will of God is a decision of the heart. Either you are all in for what is written in the Bible about Jesus Christ, or you are not. If you are not all in, then you are saying in your heart, "There is no God." It is so unfortunate how we allow our minds to be clouded with untruths.

Paul writes in 1 Timothy 4:1-3, "Now the Spirit expressly says that in latter times some will depart from the faith, giving heed to deceiving spirits and doctrines of demons, speaking lies in hypocrisy, having their own conscience seared with a hot iron, forbidding to marry, and commanding to abstain from foods which God created to be received with thanksgiving by those who believe and know the truth."

What I discovered most about the churches I used to attend is these deceiving spirits and doctrines of demons are there for the purpose of turning church members away from the truth of the Bible. People who are in the pulpit are not good ministers of the truth of God's word. Ministers have a mandate to be good ministers of Jesus Christ. (V-6) They not only have a mandate to be good ministers, but the members should see the application of Scripture taking place in their lives. Paul continues in verse 7, "But reject profane and old wives' fables and exercise yourself toward godliness." Paul warns ministers to avoid teaching on subjects that are not true and don't pertain to the truth of the gospel of Jesus Christ. We as churchgoers and church members fail to recognize false teaching because so many of us chose to return to it week after week. Agree and give affirmation to it by uttering the words "amen" "preach pastor" and "that's a good word right there" because unfortunately, we have not come into the wisdom, knowledge, and understanding of Scripture. Our hearts have not been replaced, we have not prayed like David, who asked God to give him a clean heart and to renew a right spirit within him. We have that zeal for

God but lack knowledge. We have not experienced godly sorrow because we have never come to true repentance of the sin in our lives. We are deceived by these doctrines of demons coming out of the pulpits in many of our churches, which is so unfortunate. Listen to what David prayed in Psalm 51. "Have mercy upon me, O God, according to Your lovingkindness; According to the multitude of Your tender mercies, Blot out my transgressions. Wash me thoroughly from my iniquity, And cleanse me from my sin. For I acknowledge my transgressions, And my sin is always before me. Against You, You only have I sinned, And done this evil in Your sight-That You may be found just when You speak, And blameless when You judge. Behold, You desire truth in the inward parts, And in the hidden part You will make me know wisdom. Purge me with hyssop (hyssop was used in the Old Testament to cleanse someone from their sin) and I shall be clean. Wash me, and I shall be whiter than snow. Make me hear joy and gladness, That the bones You have broken may rejoice. Hide Your face from my sins And blot out all my iniquities. Create in me a clean heart, O God, and renew a steadfast spirit within me."

David was asking God to put a new song in his heart. A song of praise and hope. He knew no one could touch his heart like God. David was experiencing something that most church members have yet to experience. He felt detached from the relationship he had developed with God because of the sins he had committed. David wanted that relationship back. He humbled himself and asked for God to clean him up. He needed to know that he was forgiven. He needed a fresh start. Even though David felt like he had lost the up close and personal relationship that he had developed with God, he knew how to get it back. As in verses 16 & 17 he says, "For You do not desire sacrifice, or else I would give it; You do not delight in burnt offering. The sacrifices of God are a broken spirit, A broken and a contrite heart-These, O God, You will not despise."

God doesn't care about rituals and traditions that take place in our church services every week. He cares about us having the right attitudes, and genuine repentance of our sins. God will not turn away someone who comes with a humble heart and someone who is willing to obey. You and I can attend church seven days a week, but it means absolutely nothing to God if there is habitual sin and disobedience to the word of God. It doesn't matter if you are in the pulpit or in the pews, obedience is better than any so-called sacrifice you think you are making for God.

The Bible expresses the importance of wisdom. Proverbs 23:23 states, "Buy the truth, and do not sell it, Also wisdom and instruction and understanding." We must do all we can, with the help of the Holy Spirit, because He is a helper, to obtain all the wisdom, knowledge, and understanding of the truth of God's word and make every effort to apply it to our everyday lives. The mysteries of salvation are hidden from most churchgoers because they don't believe the truths of the gospel. Disobedience is at an all-time high in the church. And if disobedience remains in the church, God will continue to allow the devil to have his way in the lives of most church members.

The disciples in Matthew chapter 13 asked Jesus why He spoke in parables. In verse 13 He said, "Therefore I speak to them in parables, because seeing they do not see, and hearing they do not hear, nor do they understand." Jesus was quoting Isaiah 6:9,10. Jesus went on to say in 14b,15 "Hearing you will hear and shall not understand And seeing you will see and not perceive; For the hearts of this people have grown dull. Their ears are hard of hearing, And their eyes have been closed, Lest they should see with their eyes and hear with their ears, Lest they should understand with their hearts and turn, So that I should heal them." This is a heart issue.

Down through the centuries, man has not had a heart for God. For most people, God is just a passing thought, and He knows it. If you didn't know,

God is all-knowing. We go to church and participate in the rituals and traditions without knowing that God is looking at our hearts, examining our thoughts, and knowing who is real and who is a pretender. Most church members today don't want to commit to the truth of the gospel of Jesus Christ. They just want to go through the motions, because they're hearts, and minds are far from the Lord and there is no fear of Him. Which leads to a lack of wisdom, knowledge, and understanding. I close this chapter with a prayer from Psalm 85:

"You have taken away all Your wrath; You have turned from the fierceness of Your anger. Restore us, O God of our salvation, And cause Your anger toward us to cease. Will You be angry with us forever? Will You prolong Your anger to all generations? Will You not revive us again, That Your people may rejoice in You? Show us Your mercy, Lord, And grant us Your salvation I will hear what God the Lord will speak, For He will speak peace To His people and to His saints; But let them not turn back to folly. Surely His salvation *is* near to those who fear Him, That glory may dwell in our land. Mercy and truth have met together; Righteousness and peace have kissed. Truth shall spring out of the earth, And righteousness shall look down from heaven. Yes, the Lord will give *what is* good; And our land will yield its increase. Righteousness will go before Him And shall make His footsteps *our* pathway."

Lack of Faith

There is a lack of faith in God in our church today and God is not pleased. In Hebrews 11:6 the Bible says, "But without faith, it is impossible to please Him, for he who comes to God must believe that He is, and that He is a rewarder of those who diligently seek Him." God is very serious about faith. The gospel reveals to us that it is faith and by faith alone, we come to a holy God. "The just shall live by faith." (Habakkuk 2:4; Romans 1:17) "Faith is the substance of things hope for, the evidence of things not seen." (Hebrews 11:1) A just man lives by his faith; he's expecting a change to come no matter how long it takes. When we as children of God diligently seek Him, we discover that God can only be approached by faith. It is only the righteousness of Jesus Christ that allows our sinful nature to come into the present of a holy God. That's why we cannot allow sin to have dominion in our lives.

Faith set us apart from the faithless.

"Therefore, having been justified by faith, we have peace with God through our Lord Jesus Christ." (Romans 5:1) When Jesus died on the cross, we were reconciled with God. Instead of God fighting against us, He is fighting for us. That's why when we come to God, we have no other choice but to believe that He is who He says He is. That can only happen through faith. If we lack faith in God, we put our faith in something other than God. We all have faith in something. If we work a job, we have faith that on payday, we will receive a paycheck. When we go to our vehicles and put the key in or push a button, we have faith that it is going to start. When we sit in a chair, we have faith that it will hold us up and not break. When we hit the light switch, we have faith that the lights will come on. We place faith in things we can see, touch, hear, feel, and taste. People lack faith in God because they cannot see Him, they cannot touch Him, they never hear His voice, they cannot smell Him, they can't fill or taste Him. That's why Hebrews tells us, that faith is the evidence of things not seen. We believe in and have faith in our houses, cars, politicians, athletes, schools, fake news reports. We believe that the things we eat will not harm us, even though most of the things we choose to eat can be harmful to our health. We have faith and take for granted that the person preparing the meal is a clean Chef and a good cook. We have faith that he/she will not put anything in the food that would harm us. If we only had that kind of faith in an Almighty God.

"Therefore, having been justified by faith, we have peace with God through our Lord Jesus Christ." (Romans 5:1) Therefore, having been justified means to be declared innocent or guiltless, acquitted from all our sins. Some people find that hard to believe. That's why it must be done by faith. The problem with people inside and outside the church is that they have never physically seen God, therefore they don't believe in Him. They talk a good God game, but their actions tell you something totally different. When you accept Jesus Christ as your Savior, the Holy Spirit comes along as part of the package. Remember salvation is a gift. "We are saved by grace through faith, and not of yourselves; it is a gift of God, not of works, least, anyone should boast." (Ephesians 2:8) As we unwrap that gift, there is something very important inside, that so many Christian leave in the box. It's the Holy Spirit. With the Holy Spirit comes the power and courage to believe. The Bible makes the gospel so easy to understand that most people, without even realizing it say to themselves, this is too good to be true and they don't believe. Instead of belief and the transforming of their hearts and minds, doubt kicks in and it causes so many people in the church to miss out on all God has for them. "For we are His workmanship created in Christ Jesus for good works," (Ephesians 2:10a) not church works. That's why when a little tribulation comes along, we crumble under the pressure. The Holy Spirit filled Christian glory in tribulation because Romans 5:3-5 states, "but we glory in tribulations, knowing that tribulation produces perseverance; and perseverance, character; and character, hope. Now hope does not disappoint, because the love of God has been poured out in our hearts by the Holy Spirit who was given to us."

There are too many unregenerate Christians/churchgoers who are spiritually dead and have not been made alive by the power of the Holy Spirit in the pews and pulpits of the church. Romans 5:8-11, "But God demonstrated His love toward us, in that while we were still sinners, Christ died for us. Much more then, having now been justified by His blood, we shall be saved from wrath through Him. For if we were enemies we were reconciled to God through the death of His Son, much more, having been reconciled, we shall be saved by His life." And not only that, but we also rejoice in God through our Lord Jesus Christ, through whom we have now received reconciliation." Wrath is coming on the children of disobedience. And there is a lot of disobedience and lack of faith in the church. There must come a time in the life of a professed believer that they realize the importance of practicing righteous. That is what separates the children of God and the children of the devil. "We are all God's children." That is a false statement. God does love all people because God so loved the world that he gave the life of Jesus Christ for all of us. But 1 John 3 put it in perspective. V-1 "Behold what manner of love the Father has bestowed on us that we should be called children of God!" V-4 "Whoever commits sin also commits lawlessness, and sin is lawlessness." V-7-10 "Little children, let no one deceive you. He who practices righteousness is righteous, just as He (Jesus) is righteous. He who sins is of the devil, for the devil has sinned from the beginning. For this purpose, the Son of God was manifested, that He might destroy the works of the devil. Whoever is born of God does not sin, for His seed remains in him; and he cannot sin, because he is born of God. In this the children of God and the children of the devil are manifest: Whoever does not practice righteousness is not of God, nor is he who does not love his brother." That means if you are still practicing habitual sin and you have hate in your heart, this is strong evidence that salvation has never taken place in your life. You have been led astray, deceived, fooled into believing something that is not true.

There are so many church members who are still under the influence of the devil and have not experienced the new birth.

We know that whoever is born of God does not sin, but he who has been born of God keeps himself, and the wicked one does not touch him. We know that we are of God, and the whole world lies under the sway of the wicked one. 1 John 5:18-19

Conformation of the new birth comes from the Spirit Himself. Looking at 1 John 3:10b it tells us if we don't love our brother that we are not practicing righteousness. When we don't express love to other believers, the Bible says we don't even know God. 1 John 4:8 tells us, "He who does not love does not know God, for God is love." The evidence of a person being a born-again Christian is seen in their ability to show love. It is a part of who true believers are. It is obedience by faith. We must always obey Scripture, regardless of how we feel. The world system, which is ruled and created by the devil, is always putting pressure on us to disobey God and satisfy our flesh. When we practice righteousness by faith and believe in God, He gives us the power to overcome this world system. 1 John 5:4-5, "For whatever is born of God overcomes the world. And this is the victory that has overcome the world—our faith. Who is he who overcomes the world, but he who believes that Jesus is the Son of God?" Faith in Jesus Christ gives us the power to overcome this evil system which is played out in the lives of unbelievers. "Faith is the key, so don't stop believing. In Him you'll find a love that stays close by." These are the lyrics to a song sung by Alvin Slaughter.

The Bible says, "We walk by faith, not by sight" (2 Corinthians 5:7) The more we learn, how to practice walking by faith, the more we place our confidence in God and not ourselves. We not only walk by faith, the Bible says, "The just shall live by faith; But if anyone draws back, my soul has no pleasure in them." (Hebrews 10:38) You don't want to be one who falls back into a state of spiritual ruin, a loss soul, which leads to hell.

The problem with most of those who turn back is there is a lack of commitment, a lack of faith in God and His word. Most people just don't want to be all in for Jesus Christ. In Alabama and across the country people put their faith in the Alabama Crimson Tide football team. People come out by the tens of thousands to watch an Alabama football game, while millions watch on television. Alabama fans are so committed that the thought of being anywhere else on a Saturday, in the fall, other than at the game or watching on television, is totally out of the question. The thought of missing a game does not even enter the thought process of an Alabama football fan. They are in total disbelief if they happen to be on the losing end of a game. They enter every game with much confidence that they are going to come out of each game with a win. Now if Alabama football fans can have that much faith in a football team that has created nothing but an ungodly environment to watch a football game, how much more should we as Christians, churchgoers, or followers of the Lord Jesus Christ make a commitment to live a life of faith to a God who created the universe. The Alabama football fan is all in for the team. Fans are so dedicated and put forth so much effort to support the Crimson Tide, and there is no shame when it comes to letting everyone know who and what they believe in. Christians have for too long shown a lack of confidence and faith in our Lord and Savior Jesus Christ. The Lord who gave His life on the cross that we might live. Colossians 1:13-14 tells us some of the results of what happened on that cross. "He has delivered us from the power of darkness and conveyed us into the kingdom of the Son of His love, in whom we have redemption through His blood, the forgiveness of sins."

It is good to know that we can place our faith in the words written in Scripture. Faith in knowing that we have been redeemed, set free from the bondage of sin by the blood that Jesus shed. To be washed in the blood and forgiven for our past, present, and future sins.

Lack of Understanding

Buy the truth, and do not sell it, Also wisdom and instruction and understanding. Proverbs 23:23 There is a lack of understanding in the church of the basic fundamentals of the gospel of Jesus Christ. The reason why there is a lack of understanding is that most of us in the church are spiritually dead. There are some who will attend church all their lives and still have not come to an understanding of living the Christian life and receiving all the benefits of what God has for those who learn and practice the faith.

Far more than anything else, a spiritually dead person needs to be made alive by God. Salvation brings spiritual life to the dead. The same power that raised Jesus from the dead is the same power that is made available for all those who believe and understand the importance of living this Christian life. This power energizes and makes the spiritually dead alive. It's only the grace of God that saves us from the Wrath to come. Becoming alive transfers a person from one sphere to another.

"And you, He made alive, who were dead in trespasses and sins, in which you once walked according to the course of this world, according to the prince of the power of the air, the spirit who now works in the sons of disobedience, among whom also we once conducted ourselves in the lust of our flesh, fulfilling the desires of the flesh and of the mind, and were by nature children of wrath, just as the others. But God, who is rich in mercy, because of His great love with which He loved us, even when we were dead in trespasses, made us alive together with Christ (by grace you have been saved), and raised us up together, and made us sit together in the heavenly places in Christ Jesus, that in the age to come He might show the exceeding riches of His grace in His kindness toward us in Christ Jesus. (Ephesians 2:1-7)

Now that was a lot for us to chew on. And if you are spiritually dead, you cannot even start to understand the rich knowledge in these seven verses. Paul is reminding people who are saved about the richness of God's grace and mercy. He is speaking in the past tense. Verse 1, "And you, He made alive, who were dead" Verse 2 "in which you once walked" Verse 3 "among whom also we all once conducted ourselves, Verse 4 and were by nature, just as the others" Verse 5 "even when we were dead; made us alive; you have been saved" Verse 6 "raised us up, made us sit," and Verse 7 ends up stating, "in Christ Jesus."

So, what is a spiritually dead person? A spiritually dead person is anyone who does not have a serious relationship with God the Father through our Lord Jesus Christ. We as human beings are born that way. You don't come into this world loving anybody or anything but yourself. That is why Jesus says in John 3:3, "You must be born again. It is a spiritual awakening. You are made alive by God Himself to the reality of what life is all about."

Life is all about holy living, praising the name of the Lord Jesus Christ, and giving God thanks for the goodness that is going on in your life. You are not only to praise Him when things are going well, but you praise God even in difficult times.

"I will bless the Lord at all times, His praise shall continually be in my mouth." (Psalm 34:1) I have learned in my life, that regardless of what a person may be going through, it could always be worse.

When you are made alive by God, you die at the same time. Die to what? Sin. You die to the sin in your life. "For He who has died has been freed from sin. Now if we died with Christ, we believe that we shall also live with Him." (Romans 6:7-8) Once you understand that Jesus Christ has been raised from the dead and that you receive the revelation that you will not die again, death no longer has power over you. Even though all of us are born through our mother's womb, we are all spiritually dead. So, until you are born again, you are a dead man walking, sentenced to death, eternal death, in the lake of fire with the devil and his angels. "But God who is rich in mercy, because of His great love for us, even when we were dead in trespasses and sin, made us alive together with Christ (by grace you have been saved through faith). Ephesians 2:4-5

Let's talk about trespasses. The definition for trespasses is to go beyond the limits of what is considered right; to do wrong; a moral offense; to transgress: which means to break a law or command. The MacArthur commentary states, "It is a sobering reminder to Christians of the total sinfulness and lostness from which believers have been redeemed. It indicates the realm or sphere in which ungenerated

sinners exist. They are not dead because of sinful acts that have been committed, but because of their sinful nature." Because in verse 2 Paul writes, "In which you once walked according to the course of this world according to the prince of the air, the spirit that is now working in the son of disobedience." In which you once walked, is a phrase used in the past tense. Once walked tells me that I have been delivered from a life of trespasses and sin. You have to, if you are born again. Paul continues in verse 3, "among whom also we all once conducted ourselves in the lust of the flesh, fulfilling the desires of the flesh and of the mind, and were by nature children of wrath, just as the others." Sin does negative things to us and others. If sin were positive or even neutral, a loving God would be unconcerned about it. He would not lead us to repentance, which is far more than a mere change of mind or remorse. Repentance involves a turning from sin to God, which results in righteous living. Genuine repentance is a work of God in the human heart. If sin were not bad for us, God would not lead us to repentance or demand that we repent of it. He would not command us to overcome it and come out of this world. Jesus commanded the adulterous woman in John 8:11 to go and sin no more. In John 5:14, the man who was at the pool for 38 years waiting to be healed and after Jesus healed the man He said, "See you have been made well. Sin no more, lest a worse thing come upon you." The same message or commandment is the same for us once we are born again. "Go and sin no more."

When you talk about sin, you must start with the founder of it. His name is Satan, which means adversary. He is against God, and anything godly. His name means destroyer. Satan is a destroyer, and the spirit that emanates from him drives this world and produces sin. It is a destroying spirit. We can boldly say that sin does two bad things simultaneously: it produces negative results and destroys. If humans exist, we will never be able to retire the acts of sin that exist in all our lives. None of us are perfect; we all sin on occasion, and certainly, sin affects all of us, both when we sin and when others sin. The word itself, however, is so commonly used that it has become debased, (which means to become lower in value) distorted, and abused. In this condition, it carries little emotional and intellectual force. To some people, it has become like a fairy tale: "The Sky is Falling" of Chicken Little Fame. To unbelievers, sin is almost a joke. They even compose songs containing light and heavy lyrics in reference to sin. Largely, the world only recognizes the most obvious sins like murder, stealing, rape, and many others that we think are awful because they lack understanding of what the Bible teaches on sin, and they lack knowledge about this sinful nature that can only be tamed by the Holy Spirit.

Then we have carnal Christians who live by sight, not by faith, and the effects of sin are not always immediately discernible. They do not understand the negative fruit that also results from being a carnal-minded Christian and they are unable to pick up on the less obvious sins because of a lack of discernment.

For though by this time, you ought to be teachers, you need someone to teach you again the first principles of the oracles of God, and you come to need milk and not solid food. For everyone who partakes only of milk is unskilled in the word of righteousness, for he is a babe. But solid food belongs to those who are of full age, that is, those who by reason of use have their senses exercised to discern both good and evil. Hebrews 5:12-14 Christians who practice sin lack discernment. They are practicing sin which makes them a child of the devil. 1 John 3:8

So, the question on the floor is what are you as a churchgoer practicing? Do you understand the importance of practicing righteousness as opposed to continuing with the practices of the sinful nature? Far too many people who attend church allow their flesh to get in the way of having spiritual success. It is so easy to get caught up in pleasing people instead of pleasing God. A lot of us don't understand what is at stake when we continue taking our lives in the direction of this world system. In other words, we continue to work on our relationship with the world and do not work on our relationship with our Lord and Savior Jesus Christ. We must make a choice. We can't follow God and follow the world's way of doing things at the same time. God is so kind and loving, and He wants us to experience His best. If we fulfill the desires of this sinful nature, we will never be able to taste the goodness of God. More important than that is people who choose to fulfill the desires of a sinful nature will have no part in the kingdom of God.

When we make up our minds to walk with God, Galatians 5:22 tells us there is a fruit produced by the Holy Spirit. That fruit is love, joy, peace, patience, kindness, goodness, faithfulness, gentleness, and self-control. This fruit allows us to operate at a high level spiritually when placed in situations where this fruit is needed. When you are walking with God you are walking in the Spirit, which will prevent you from fulfilling the desires of the flesh or satisfying your sinful nature. The spirit enables you to love the unlovable, experience peace in the storms of life, practice patience when you feel rushed, be kind to those who hate and mistreat you, be good to those who may not deserve or appreciate your goodness, place all your faith and trust in God even when you can't see or know the outcome of a situation. To be tenderhearted not severe or rough when a situation or person needs to see a gentle side, and to have self-control and not allow your flesh to be in control, which could lead to regret.

In 1 John Chapter 5, the apostle wants us to understand who Jesus is. "And we know that the Son of God has come and has given us an understanding, that we may know Him who is true, in His Son Jesus Christ. This is the true God and eternal life." (4:20) Then he writes in verse 21, "Little children, keep yourselves from idols."

I am not amazed at the lack of understanding in the church. Most churchgoers don't realize that Jesus Christ came to give us an understanding of who God is and the importance of knowing Him. He is not just the Son of God, but He is God, and He came for the purpose of giving us eternal life. The problem is that most of us who attend church have put other gods in His place. We care more about having a relationship with the world than we do with the God of heaven. Satan, the prince of the air, has blinded us. Not only has he blinded us, but he has strategically placed weak-minded men and women in places of authority with very little to no knowledge of Scripture to point members to idols instead of the living God Jesus Christ.

Church has become a multibillion-dollar business and people are emotionalized instead of convicted of their sins and sinful lifestyles. When was the last time you attended a church service and heard a message on repentance? Jesus Christ's first sermon in Mark 1:15, "The time is fulfilled, and the kingdom of God is at hand. Repent and believe the gospel." Peter, I Acts 2:38, "Repent, and let every one of you be baptized in the name of Jesus Christ for the remission of sins; and you shall receive the gift of the

Holy Spirit." In verse 40, Peter exhorted them saying, "Be saved from this perverse generation."

The church has become dull of hearing. When you become dull of hearing you have no need to try to understand the deep things of God. God is not like us. He is infinite, we are finite. God is eternal, we are temporal. God has no beginning. God has no end. There is a set time for a human being to be born, then they die. And as it is appointed for men to die once, but after this the judgment. Hebrews 9:27

"Seek the Lord while He may be found, Call upon Him, while He is near. Let the wicked forsake his way, And the unrighteous man his thoughts; Let him return to the Lord, And He will have mercy on him; And to our God, For He will abundantly pardon. For My thoughts are not your thoughts, Nor are your ways My ways, says the Lord. For as the heavens are higher than the earth, So are My ways higher than your ways, And My thoughts higher than your thoughts." Isaiah 55:6-9

We can't even start to comprehend a God who is full of grace and mercy. We may not be able to comprehend the God of heaven but that should not detour us from seeking the understanding that we need to take God and His word seriously. James writes, "Who is wise and understanding among you? Let him show by good conduct that his works are done in the meekness of wisdom." James 3:13

There are two important sections of Scripture that we must understand. Judgment is coming. This is not the time to misunderstand the importance of the cross and the fact that judgment will begin in the church.

For the time has come for judgment to begin at the house of God; and if it begins with us first, what will be the end of those who do not obey the gospel of God? If the righteous are scarcely saved, Where will the ungodly and the sinner appear?

1 Peter 4:17-18

There are too many people who attend church but do not understand the importance of obedience. Too many people, who act like they are involved in a relationship with the Father, through His Son Jesus Christ. We love sin and we practice unrighteousness. We are hearers and not doers of the word of God. Therefore lay aside all filthiness and overflow of wickedness, and receive with meekness the implanted word, which is able to save your soul. But be doers of the word and not hearers only, deceiving yourselves. James 1:21-22 Too many churchgoers are self-deceived.

Dear friends, if we deliberately continue sinning after we have received knowledge of the truth, there is no longer any sacrifice that will cover these sins. There is only the terrible expectation of God's judgment and the raging fire that will consume his enemies. For anyone who refused to obey the law of Moses was put to death without mercy on the testimony of two or three witnesses. Just think how much worse the punishment will be for those who have trampled on the Son of God, and have treated the blood of the covenant, which made us holy, as if it were common and unholy, and have insulted and disdained the Holy Spirit who brings God's mercy to us. For we know the one who said, "I will take revenge. I will pay them back." He also said, "The LORD will judge his own people." Hebrews 10:26-30

We lack understanding of the importance of what happened on the cross. The blood that was poured out of the body of our Lord and Savior Jesus Christ. The horrific death. The suffering. The ultimate sacrifice. He did it so we might have eternal life. Do we really think that God will forgive any of us for insulting the cross through our disobedience? He tells us He will punish people for the wrongs they do; I will repay them. And He also said, "The Lord will judge His people. Jesus Christ died for the sins of the world. Every sin that was ever committed, and every sin that will ever be committed. God is not willing that any should perish but that all should come to repentance." 2 Peter 3:9b

You need to understand that you are not your own. For you have been bought with a price; therefore, glorify God in your body and in your spirit, which is God's. For He can destroy not only our bodies but also our souls.

The spirit of formality

As I begin this last chapter, I want to get to the root of the problem in our church services today. The root of the problem is a spirit of formality. The major reason why most churches and the services that are conducted and orchestrated stinks is because we control the order of the service, and we don't leave room for the working of the Holy Spirit. What is formality? It is a condition or quality of being formal; in accordance with what's required or its traditional, rules, and procedures; it is conventionally rigorous. When a methodical system is put in place. When you establish a particular order.

We have this attitude in most of our church services, 'this is the way we conduct our services, and we are not open to change. It seems like there is this attitude which is teetering on a boldness or cockiness without even knowing it. An attitude that we are not open to change, and we don't have any spiritual insight to recognize that what we are doing in our church services saddens God. We start at an appointed time and our own goal is to end our services at a particular time. Again, the idea is to please and satisfy men and not God. Now there is nothing wrong with starting a church service on time, if it is done for the right reason. Church service may last anywhere from 45 minutes to 3 hours. It just depends on who is in charge of the service. Some church services are a little longer, and some are a little shorter. There is no anticipation of a move of the Holy Spirit on the hearts of those in attendance. People who attend church have allowed themselves to be influenced by the commandments, philosophies, traditions, and doctrines of men.

"Beware lest anyone cheat you through philosophy and empty deceit, according to the tradition of men, according to the basic principles of the world, and not according to Christ."

Colossians 2:8

Jesus tells the religious leaders they had made the commandments of God of no effect by their traditions.

Matthew 15:6

Jesus explains in verse 7; These people draw near to Me with their mouth And honor Me with their lips, But their heart is far from Me. In vain they worship Me, Teaching as doctrines the commandments of men.

Jesus continues to warn us about these religious leaders, 21st century preachers, so-called teachers, and pastors. "Let them alone. They are blind leaders of the blind. And if the blind leads the blind, both will fall into a ditch." Matthew 15:14

I found myself in the past sitting in church services described by Jesus. If the Spirit of God had not led me to get out, my family and I would be on our way to that ditch. It is a ditch that causes a person to fall further and further away from Bible doctrine. I was deceived. It is so unfortunate that covid-19 gave these pastors another way to make money. Another way to spread this false doctrine to present to more people this 21st century jesus. In 2020, social media church service was created. When covid-19 came out of nowhere, everything was shut down, except Walmart, Lowe's, Home Depot and a few other retailers, who were all in on the scam. Unfortunately, even the church bowed down to this satanic movement and caved to the demands of the government, instead of standing on the word of God. This is all the evidence that is needed, if it was presented in a court case that would find the church not guilty of violating the rules and regulations of the spirit of the antichrist. You have to understand that a business needs funds to continue to operate. If everyone is ordered to stay home, and businesses have been shut down, they have to figure out a way to keep the cash flow going. Social media church services not only gave them an opportunity to collect money from their members, but also from people who could tune in to their social media services from all over the world who watch on YouTube, Facebook, Instagram, and other outlets. It was a new way of doing church business. A win-win situation for these crafty businessmen and women. So, months later as members started to slowly make their way back to church, there was a new audience on social media who could continue to watch and give funds. These people are very crafty. Making money will always be the number one priority of 95% of the church services that are held around the world.

There is so much misinformation coming from pulpits today. It's been going on for over 2000 years.

Jesus weeps over Israel, Luke 19:41-42

Now as He drew near, He saw the city and wept over it, saying "If you had known, even you, especially in this your day, the things that make for your peace! But now they are hidden from your eyes.

Jesus knew the hearts of the people. This same crowd who cheered His entry into the city in Luke 19, would call for His death in Luke 23:20-21.

Pilate, therefore, wishing to release Jesus, again called out to them. But they shouted, saying, "Crucify Him, crucify Him!

Romans 9:1-4

O Israel, my people! O, my Jewish brothers! How I long for you to come to Christ. My heart is heavy within me, and I grieve bitterly day and night because of you. Christ knows and the Holy Spirit knows that it is no mere pretense when I say that I would be willing to be forever damned if that would save you. God has given you so much but still, you do not listen to Him.

Hosea 4:6-7 TLB My people are destroyed because they don't know Me, and it is all your fault, you priest, for you refuse to know Me; therefore, I refuse to recognize you as my priest. Since you have forgotten My laws, I will forget to bless your children. The more My people multiplied, the more they sin against Me. They exchange the glory of God for the disgrace of idols.

2 Timothy 4:1-4 TLB

And so, I solemnly urge you before God and before Jesus Christ who will someday judge the living and the dead when He appears to set up His kingdom to preach the Word of God urgently at all times, whenever you get a chance, in season and out, when it is convenient and when it is not. Correct and rebuke your people when they need it, encourage them to do right, and all the time be feeding them patiently with God's Word. (3) For there is going to come a time when people won't listen to the truth but will go around looking for teachers who will tell them just what they want to hear. They won't listen to what the Bible says but will blithely follow their own misguided ideas.

That word blithely means without much thought, concern, or care.

This spirit of formality does not allow the Holy Spirit to move, to operate, to perform surgery on the hearts of those who need Him most. Remember, the heart is deceitful above all things and desperately wicked. Jerimiah 17:9 People's hearts and minds are not being changed by what they hear coming out of the mouths of these 21st century preachers. These preachers lack the courage to correct, rebuke, and encourage people to do right, to live holy, and to practice righteousness. They don't patiently feed them God's word. They are too afraid of losing members instead of losing souls. It is like a race to the top to see who can get and keep the most members. The sad part about all of this is that most members would not have it any other way.

This spirit of formality has caused the church to take a seat. A back seat in this society we live in. A society dominated by the practice and approval of sin. The lifestyle of sin is the norm in this society we live in. Compromise is promoted and tolerance is expected. We have had churches located throughout our cities, rural areas, and surrounding counties for centuries and we have not only failed to come together and get in the fight, but we have refused to come together or join forces to fight against the evil and the wickedness that is promoted and pushed down our throats 24 hours a day 7 days a week. We have focus on things that are important to us but not important to God. God only asks that we love Him and that we love one another and obey what is written in Scripture. Instead of the church impacting the world, the church has been infiltrated by the world. It is more important to grow membership, collect tithes and offerings, and build worship centers to entertain large groups of people who are on their way to hell with heaven on their minds than for these churches to save souls for the kingdom. We have men and unfortunately women in the pulpits of churches across the country who have never experienced godly sorrow which produces repentance and leads a man or woman to salvation.

We have people who have attended church all their lives and have never heard the gospel of Jesus Christ. Most people who attend church are not told to come out of the ways of this world and live for God. They are not told to live holy and practice righteousness. They are not told that the wages of sin are death but the gift of God is eternal life. Romans 6:23

I have attended church most of my life. As I look back and examine, I see there is a lack of repentence, a lack of knowledge, a lack of wisdom, a lack of understanding, a lack of holiness, a lack of self-control, a lack of love, a lack of peace, and a lack of faith in our churches. But there is no lack of sin and disobedience to Scripture.

Unfortunately, there is a lack of repentance which is needed now more than ever. Here are a few verses in the Bible that addresses the subject of repentance:

In those days John the Baptist came preaching in the wilderness of Judea and saying, Repent for the kingdom of heaven is at hand. Matthew 3:2

Now after John was put in prison, Jesus came to Galilee, preaching the gospel of the kingdom of God, and saying, "The time is fulfilled, and the kingdom of God is at hand. Repent, and believe in the gospel. Mark 1:14-15

So, they went out and preached that people should repent. Mark 6:12

I tell you, no, but unless you repent you will all likewise perish. Luke 13:5

Again, godly sorrow produces repentance leading to salvation, not to be regretted; but the sorrow of the world produces death. TLB 2 Corinthians 7:10

People don't come to salvation because they cannot come to the reality of what happened on the cross. The horrific death and how Jesus willingly paid the price to satisfy the wrath that is reserved for those who refuse to believe. Those who choose not to submit to the desire of God. His desire is that all men, not some men be saved and come to the knowledge of the truth. 1 Timothy 2:4

For He made Him who knew no sin to be sin for us, that we might become the righteousness of God in Him. 2 Corinthians 5:21

Repent therefore and be converted, that your sins may be blotted out, so that times of refreshing may come from the presence of the Lord. Acts 3:19

We get together every Sunday morning and put God on a schedule. We're looking at the preacher with that "get me out of here by 12, get me out of here by 1" look on most of our faces. We treat God like he is an employee that we want and need to show up for work but when it is time for roll call and we call out His name, Jesus, if we are honest with ourselves, we must mark Him absent because He is not in the service. He is like the teacher who calls in sick and the class needs a substitute teacher. That substitute is nobody but satan himself showing up in most church services every Sunday. People aren't getting saved, people are not growing in the grace and knowledge of our Lord and Savior, Jesus Christ and I believe it saddens the heart of God like it saddens the heart of the Apostle Paul. I'm saddened and anyone who is a true believer, a true follower of the Lord Jesus Christ should be saddened too.

When it comes to God, we have this "spare tire mentality." We keep Him in the trunk and pull God out when life goes flat. I believe we are in the last days, and I believe we may be the generation to see the return of our great Savior, Jesus Christ.

What frightens me, and what saddens me is that the fear of the Lord has departed the hearts and minds of most people who attend church. I can relate to and even understand there being no fear of God in so-called non-Christians, but Christians, people who attend church, there is no fear of a God who is able to destroy the body and the soul.

Then they will call on me, but I will not answer; They will seek me diligently, but they will not find me. Because they hated knowledge And did not choose the fear of the Lord,

Proverbs 1:28-29

There is no need to raise money to support missionaries. The 21st century church has become a large mission field that must be addressed. All of us must examine ourselves, and test ourselves to see if we are in the faith.

2 Corinthians 13:5, "Check up on yourselves. Are you really Christians? Do you pass the test? Or are you just pretending to be Christians when actually you aren't at all?

What a great and mighty God we serve. He is loving. He is full of compassion. He is patient. He is kind. He is faithful. He is magnificent. He is holy. He is righteous. He is radiant in all His glory. He is slow to anger. He is a God of love 1 John 4:16 tells us that God is love. Paul writes in Philippians 3:10, that I may know Him and the power of His resurrection, and the fellowship of His sufferings, being conformed to His death. Paul's mindset was like Jesus'. Christ died for the purpose of redeeming sinners. Paul had that same purpose in a lesser sense; he lived and would willingly put his life on the line to reach sinners with the gospel.

So, how do we defeat or combat this spirit of formality? It is so deeply rooted in our church services. It starts with corporate repentance. We must tell God that we are sorry for taking our time together for granted. The fear and reference for God that was on display in the early church, in the book of Acts, must return to our church services. It is a time to take God seriously, and not take Him for granted. We must return to the fundamentals of the gospel of Jesus Christ and appreciate the small things He has done; what He is doing and what He wants to do. We live in an evil world and Jesus is our only hope. We must recognize and acknowledge our need for Jesus. We are in a fight for our spiritual survival, so we must learn how to walk confidently in the Spirit and not allow our flesh to make spiritual decisions. We must become intentional and take our prayer life and the reading of Scripture to a new level. Consistency is the key.

When I got saved, I started hearing and reading about how good and how great God really was. How good and great He really is. And when He returns, how good and great He will be. Pastor Earl Carter said, "Jesus is the only one who has died, and He is still here, and He is coming back."

God is the one we must continue to look to in these last days. Jesus Christ the only hope for the world.

Deut. 30:15 "See I set before you today life and good, death and evil. V 16, I command you today to love the Lord your God, to walk in His ways, and to keep His commandments, His statutes, and His judgments, that you may live and multiply, and the Lord your God will bless you."

And then He warned us in verse 17. "But if your heart turns away so that you do not hear and you draw away and worship other gods and serve them, I announce to you today that you shall surely perish; you shall not prolong your days." Then He said in verse 19, "I call heaven and earth as witnesses today against you, that I set before you life and death, blessing and cursing; therefore, choose life, that you and your descendants may live." God is so good. He loves us so much. He tells us to choose life. Choose the right way to go.

As for God, His way is perfect; The word of the Lord is proven; He is a shield to all who trust in Him. For who is God except the Lord? And who is a rock except our God? It is God who arms me with strength And makes my way perfect. Psalm 18: 30-32

He is the Rock, His work is perfect; For all His ways are justice, A God of truth and without injustice; righteous and upright is He. Deuteronomy 32:4

God is that stable, unchangeable Rock who has proven to be worthy of all praise. He is the only One who can come in and turn a situation around. He is Almighty, which translates, to power beyond understanding. The only One that can soften a hardened heart of a lost human being. He not only softens it, but He turns that heart toward Him. He is the only One we can trust and the only One we should obey.

V 20 that you may love the Lord your God, that you may obey His voice, and that you may cling to Him, for He is your life and the length of your days.

Lamentations 3:22-23 Through the Lord's mercies we are not consumed, because His compassions fail not. They are new every morning; Great is Your faithfulness. V 25-26 says, The Lord is good to those who wait for Him. To the soul who seeks Him. It is good that one should wait quietly for the salvation of the Lord.

And we know that all things work together for good to those who love God, to those who are called according to His purpose. For whom He foreknew, He also predestined to be conformed to the image of His Son, that we might be the firstborn among many brethren. Moreover, whom He predestined, these He also called; whom He called, these He justified, and whom He justified, these He also glorified. What then shall we say to these things? If God is for us, who can be against us?

Romans 8:28-31

There has never been a better time to submit to the will of God. There is so much Scripture to chew on in this book. So, I'll close with Ephesians 5:6-17

Let no one deceive you with empty words, for because of these things the wrath of God comes upon the sons of disobedience. Therefore do not be partakers with them. For you were once darkness, but now *you are* light in the Lord. Walk as children of light (for the fruit of the Spirit *is* in all goodness, righteousness, and truth), finding out what is acceptable to the Lord. And have no fellowship with the unfruitful works of darkness, but rather expose *them.* For it is shameful even to speak of those things which are done by them in secret. But all things that are exposed are made manifest by the light, for whatever makes manifest is light. Therefore, He says:

"Awake, you who sleep, Arise from the dead, And Christ will give you light." See then that you walk circumspectly, not as fools but as wise, redeeming the time, because the days are evil. Therefore, do not be unwise but understand what the will of the Lord *is*.

Made in the USA
Monee, IL
17 June 2024

59575686R00059